SECOND DAUGHTER

The Story of a Slave Girl

SECOND DAUGHTER

The Story of a Slave Girl

MILDRED PITTS WALTER

Scholastic Inc.
New York

Library of Congress Cataloging-in-Publication Data

Walter, Mildred Pitts.
  Second daughter : the story of a slave girl / Mildred Pitts Walter.
    p. cm.
  Summary: Aissa, the teen-age fictional sister of Elizabeth Freeman,
struggles against a system which declares that she is property and that she is
to remain silent.
  [1. Freeman, Elizabeth, 1744–1829 — Juvenile fiction. 2. Afro-
Americans — Fiction. 3. Slavery — Fiction. 4. Massachusetts —
History — Colonial period, ca. 1600–1775 — Fiction.]   I. Title.
PZ7.W17125Se   1996
[Fic] — dc20   95-4691
                                        CIP
                                        AC

                          ISBN 0-590-48282-3

12 11 10 9 8 7 6 5 4 3 2 1   6 7 8 9/9 0 1/0
                          Printed in the U.S.A.   37
                   First Scholastic printing, February 1996

DEDICATED TO MILTON MELTZER,
who understands that American history
is the action of *all* Americans.

It is a strange freedom to go nameless up and down the streets of other minds. . . . The name is a man's watermark above which no tide can ever rise.

— *Howard Thurman*

SECOND DAUGHTER

The Story of a Slave Girl

1

Does anyone want to know how terrible it was being a slave? And how it is now to hear and see my sister's name and still remain nameless? *She had a sister and a husband.* That's all they know about me and Josiah. But everyone will forever know her as Elizabeth Freeman, or the name whites prefer to call her, "Mum Bett," while I live among others — without a name; known only as the sister. I must tell *my* story, for I, too, have a life. I, too, have a name.

On record: Elizabeth Freeman, also called Mum Bett. Born 1742. There is no record of my name, nor the date of my birth, but I am told that on the morning I was born, an icy rain was

1

falling in Claverack, Columbia County, in the state of New York. My sister, Elizabeth, whom my parents named Fatou (Fa-too), first daughter, and Olubunmi (O-loo-BOON-mee), the midwife, say that I took my time coming and when I finally arrived I screamed loud and long. Did I know that I was being born a slave? Did I know, while still in the womb, that my five brothers had recently been sold off to the dreaded South? That my father, so enraged by the sale, struck his master and was beaten and kicked to death? That my mother no longer wanted to live?

Olubunmi said at my birth, "The ancestors didn't give this child an easy journey, but they granted her special gifts. Unlike other children, this one will appear physically weak, but she'll be strong. She will suffer greatly as a slave."

My family was the property of Cornelis Hogeboom, a Dutchman, who owned a lot of land in what was then called New Amsterdam. My father made bricks in his factory; my brothers worked in his fields and herded his cattle. Cornelis was above flogging his slaves. However, when one got into a fight, stayed away too long, lost a cow, or did not make his share of bricks, the constable was called to whip him.

The whip used had fine wire plaited into the thongs to increase the pain. When the constable was called to whip my father for confronting the master, my father fought back and, defending himself, he died.

Nine days after I was born, my mother died. She lived just long enough to defy the master and perform the naming ceremony befitting a Fulani. I was named Aissa (I-sa), second daughter. Her last words were "Fatou, give your life for your sister. Never let them separate you."

It was a cold winter that year, when Fatou, still very young, became my mother. She padded me with wool, wrapped me in a scarf that had belonged to our mother, and tied me onto her back. The warmth of her body moved into mine, creating a warmth that flowed back to her. Her heartbeat mixed with mine like the rhythm of the drum. We kept each other warm.

I was passed back and forth to other slave women on the land; and Fatou and I, without the love of our family, survived. There were many women on the farm, but Olubunmi is the one I remember most and the one who speaks to me now in my dreams. Even though I was young when we were sold away from her, I still see her tending a pot hung over a fire between stones. I can now whiff that spicy smell in the mixture she brewed. On freezing mornings she gave me a cup with the words: "It's a new day, so fill your mouth with blessings from the earth."

Often I wanted to refuse, for I was not sure what she offered. But as our eyes met over her outstretched hand, I felt as if I was drawn to do whatever she asked. When I took the cup, my hands were warmed. Steam drifted up to my nose and I was surprised at the smell of a mixture of sweet herbs and bitter roots. I drank. Warmth spread through my little body and I was able to withstand the most icy cold.

Olubunmi, a Yoruba, whose name means *this highest gift is mine,* was old. Her clothes always looked as old as she — worn, but clean. Her skin, as dark as the night, was without wrinkles, and her eyes were like black violets in a clear pool. Her liquid stare seemed able to penetrate secrets deep inside and see what ordinary eyes could not see.

It was she who encouraged storytelling around the fire at night. I can still remember the tales of the long camel caravans that came into her town bringing fabric, beads, copper, even salt. Her mother sold the thirsty tradesmen fruit, fruit juices, carob cakes, and millet fritters. Olubunmi could make me see streets alive with merchants, laughing children darting between donkeys, and water carriers.

Other women told stories and sang songs, too, but none like Olubunmi. Once while remembering Africa, she broke down and cried, longing for her family and home. I loved her, and when she hugged me close her sour odor, like burnt leaves and spices, was strange but not offensive.

Even before I was born she had taken Fatou under her wing and declared her the one who, like Olubunmi, would become a midwife and healer. Olubunmi and my sister would often slip away to gather herb leaves and roots without the master's knowing. Many times she insisted that Fatou go with her to attend the sick and to deliver babies. Because Olubunmi was both honored and feared, Baas Hogeboom did not often interfere with her activities. When we became orphans, it was Olubunmi who took charge of me and Fatou.

I remember a day of great excitement when I was about five years old. Fatou held my face in her hands and said, "A white man, Colonel John Ashley, they say from Massachusetts, has

just come here with a large herd of cattle."
There was fear in her eyes and in her voice. I
tried to remove my face from her hands, but
she held on. "Listen to me," she continued.
"This man wants to marry the baas's daughter,
Meesteres Annetje, and buy some of us."

Surrounded by older women to whom I always listened, I knew a lot about slavery, especially the word *buy*. I began to cry.

Fatou, a strong, tall girl, picked me up and
held me close. "You don't have to be scared.
I'll never let them sell us apart. Never!" She
dried my face and left me with the other children in the yard.

The place continued to hum with excitement,
but Fatou remained quiet even around Olubunmi. She talked to no one but Brom, another
slave who was like our brother. Not quite six
feet tall, Brom had a narrow brown face. When
he arrived in Claverack his hair had been long
and braided. But Hogeboom cut his braids,
leaving his hair with little peaks standing about
his head. He was a little older than Fatou, and
after our brothers were sold he claimed me and
her as his sisters.

Secretly, they put their heads together and
whispered in Fulfulde, our language that the

master forbade us to speak. If they had been caught speaking together in any language other than Dutch, they would have been whipped by the constable and one of them would have been sold. Olubunmi often worried about Fatou and Brom. "Why do you risk your hide and even being sold down the river?" she often asked.

"To speak my mother tongue gives me a pleasure worth being beaten for. And who'll know? Will you tell?" Of course Olubunmi would never tell. But she threatened to punish Fatou if ever Fatou let me hear one word, for fear I would speak it openly and lose some of my skin on the whip.

Much of the excitement was about the wedding of Meesteres Annetje to Colonel Ashley. He wanted to give his bride a slave for a wedding gift. He wanted her to have someone familiar and trustworthy. Hogeboom offered to sell the colonel Fatou. This pleased Meesteres Annetje, but Fatou was not happy. Meesteres Annetje was moody and selfish, and, because I was a weakling who was spoiled with too much pampering by old women, she did not care for me at all. She declared I was the embodiment of the devil.

Fatou knew that the master would do as he

pleased, but knowing that she would rather die
than leave me, she went to talk to him. "Baas
Hogeboom, I'm grateful that you want me to
serve our Meesteres Annetje, but please, baas,
I can't leave my little sister."

"You will if I say so and if your Meesteres
Annetje so chooses."

"I pray you don't make me go away. I can't,
and I won't go without her."

Colonel Ashley knew that his bride had her
mind set on Fatou, and that Fatou was determined to starve herself to death if she had to
leave me. He decided to buy me, too. When
he looked at the men, to choose one of them,
he chose Brom. The colonel paid forty pounds
for Brom, fifteen for Fatou, and eight for me.

I wondered what would happen to us as I
watched the tears roll down Fatou's face while
she put our things in a strong wooden box that
our father had made. She packed our mother's
scarf that she had wrapped me in to carry me
on her back; our mother's dark skirt and white
blouse that the meesteres had given her; a bon-
net and some soft shoes with tiny beads, a gift
from a woman who lived in the forest; wooden
shoes and a homespun dress and coats that each
of us had received from the baas. Carefully she

also wrapped roots and leaves and placed them in a basket.

It didn't dawn upon me that I was leaving, until I had to say good-bye to Olubunmi. I screamed and cried and clung to her as the baas pulled me away and firmly placed me in the cart that was filled with boxes, crates, and bags — gifts for Meesteres Annetje. Olubunmi cried aloud as she followed us until the new baas made her return to the farm. Fatou held me close and our tears wet our clothes.

2

For many weeks we rode and walked along streams, through green valleys, thick forests, and over mountain trails. Then one day Fatou aroused me from weary sleep; we had arrived in a place near Sheffield, Massachusetts. The valley of the Housatonic River spread before a child's eye a beauty that I could never have imagined. Among the evergreen pines and spruce trees the yellow and gold leaves of the aspens shimmered in the distance. As we descended into the valley the guide pointed out high hills and Mount Bushnell, and the tall towers of Mount Everett east of us. On the lower slopes the red, yellow, and brown leaves of the birch, oak, and sugar maple trees brightened the valley.

We wound our way down into that beautiful valley to Sheffield, a street city. Finally we came to a house made of planks instead of bricks like the one we left in Claverack. It was a well-built, big house that hugged the shore of the dark, slow-moving Housatonic River that wound through the plain.

I remember the people who came to greet us. The baas and meesteres were swept up by many from the village. They all called him master and her Mistress Anna and so we began to call him master and her Mistress Anna, too. Not as many dark faces as we knew at Baas Hogeboom's were in this place. Here, there were many more African men than women. Only two women: Sarah and Nance. The older one, Nance, was short and plump and her smile, which showed more gums than teeth, was warm and genuine. She took one look at Fatou and said, "Yo' looks. Ah thinks maybe Ah know you befo'."

"But where?" I asked in a language more Dutch than English. Sarah, younger than Nance but older than Fatou, looked at me, surprised that I should speak so to Nance.

"Oh, Ah oft' time think dat when Ah see mah kinfolk in dis land far from home. Ah look at

'em and wonder, is she from mah village? Or,
is he mah brother's son who was stole in a raid
and done come a slave of a Mande whose daughter he married? Us Af'icans is like li'l seeds that
float in de air far 'way and land close to de other
not knowin' dey from de same pod."

I had heard the women back in Claverack say
similar things and, remembering, I said, "And
you could marry your clan brother, right?"

"Aissa!" Fatou called. I saw the alarmed look
on Sarah's and Nance's faces and wondered
what I had said wrong. "She talks too much,"
Fatou sighed.

"I would say she hears one thing and understands ten," Sarah said, and laughed.

"I wuz ramblin'," Nance said. "G'wan, git yo'
things and come wid me."

We soon learned that Sarah did not belong
to the house. She was free, lived in the village,
and hired herself out as a seamstress, cook, and
housekeeper. However, when the greetings
had died away, it was Sarah who picked me up
and took me into the cellar, gave me a good
scrubbing, and dressed me in clothes that were
much too big. When Fatou had bathed herself,
the clothes she wore were much too small. They
had not expected such a big, tall girl.

I waited in the very large keeping room, or kitchen, while Fatou went with Nance to see the rest of the house. A fireplace covered a whole wall. Many iron pots and brass kettles hung on or near it. There were tables and cupboards. One table in the center of the floor had one side folded; on the other side was a drawer that looked like a shiny half barrel underneath with a round button on it near the tabletop. I grabbed the button and pulled. The shiny part was filled with flour used for making bread.

Beautiful, bright blue-and-white dishes filled a cupboard near the fireplace. I had just climbed onto a low chair nearby to see them better when the mistress entered the room. Not saying a word, she lifted me from the chair, took me into a corner, and forced me down on my bottom so hard that I let out a yell. Quickly, she put her hand over my mouth and nose. I struggled to breathe, but her grasp tightened. I bit her.

She tried to let go, but I held on and my sharp teeth cut into the palm of her hand. She screamed for help and the master came, followed by Fatou and Nance. Nance ran to the mistress and placed a cloth over her bloody hand. From the hearth, the master grabbed one of the green sticks on which the pots were hung over the flame. Fatou seeing his anger, cried, "Oh, master, wait, wait, I'll take the blame. I don't know why she did this, but it's my fault." Fatou looked frightfully scared.

The master didn't wait. He whipped me on my backside and legs until I could no longer feel the pain. After putting the stick aside, he and the mistress left the room. Both Nance and Fatou looked at me and cried. I felt so ashamed. My first day in this big house and I had made my sister and new friend cry. What had I done for the mistress to want me not to breathe?

"Oh, *mijn zusje* [my little sister]," Fatou cried. "What did you do? Do you want to be sold away from me? I can't keep you if you are not a good girl. We're servants to the master and mistress; you had better remember that."

"I only wanted to see the dishes," I cried.

"You bes learn dat de mistis is boss in dis house," Nance said. "Never, never, harm the mistis if you want tuh live."

Fatou took me to our room. She rummaged in a basket and came out with some roots and leaves that she pounded. Then she bathed my sore bottom and legs and put on them the plaster of roots and leaves. After she had covered me with a homespun cloth, she gave me a drink that made me drowsy. I remember her picking me up, but I don't remember being put in the bed I shared with her.

Fatou and I slept in a building that adjoined the house. Our room and Nance's and those of all the other slaves were in that same building. Its slanting roof made low ceilings, and only thin walls divided our space from the others. Even though our room was just big enough for our small bed and the basket and box Fatou had packed for the journey, we were glad to be together.

Fatou's tea made me sleep for two whole days. I awoke with not too much pain from the beating. Fatou stood over me. "Wake up. The master wants to see us."

She hurriedly dressed me, washed my face, and pulled me along to the big house. The mistress met us at the kitchen door, "Your master wants to speak to you, girl, not this wretched child."

Before Fatou could answer, I said, "She can listen to him better if her mind is not on me."

"Please, meesteres." Fatou spoke softly and evenly.

Mistress Anna gave in and led us up steep

stairs into a big room with high windows that let in light but, even in the day, lamps were lit. A long table had chairs around it. The walls, the color of honey, were shiny like the big dark desk behind which the master sat. A fire sparkled in a fireplace right next to a glassed-in cupboard that held fancy glasses and pitchers.

The master looked at us briefly and returned to a paper in front of him. "From this day you, the older, will bear the Christian name Bett, and you, the younger one, will be called Lizzie. You will not be called by the heathen names Fatou and Aissa ever again."

I started to speak, but Fatou squeezed hard on my shoulder as she said, "Kind master, I like the name Bett, but can I please call my sister by the name our mother gave her?"

"I have given the two of you honorable Christian names. You will be called by those names and none other. Now, I do not like to punish my servants but, as you know, I will not hesitate to do so if you do not respect your mistress and abide by the rules of this house. Bett and Lizzie, you may go."

From that day, others called me Lizzie. In the thin four walls of our room, secretly, I remained Aissa.

3

The days went by. Snow covered the hills and the rising towers of Mount Everett far away to the east. When the morning chores were done, Bett and I were free to explore the place. I shivered as we walked around, Bett looking for the herbs and roots that must grow here, too. We discovered many things on the land, among them beautiful white rocks that Nance called the cobble. The sound of Ashley Falls could not be heard because the noise of the saws and planes of the master's lumber mill filled the surrounding areas. Both black and white men were working there.

I stayed close to Bett as I walked past, near the white men. Their long hair was unkempt, their light eyes deep in their heads. I had never seen such faces — some sad, some mean, and others with eyes that reflected nothing. All were dressed alike in homespun jackets and leather trousers; the blacks seemed better cared for than the whites.

One day, Josiah Freeman, a black man, stopped his work and came to speak to us. Later I learned he was called Freeman because he was not a slave, but a free man. More than six feet tall, he was not muscular, but well built. He wore his mahogany hair in locks. His dark skin was smooth and his face hairless. He had a deep voice and a stern look, but when he spoke his smile showed strong, even white teeth.

Fatou lowered her eyes, as if lost for words. She stood with her hands down, her fingers interlocked.

"You do have a name, don't you?" Josiah asked.

"Her name's Fatou. Mine is Aissa."

Fatou quickly placed a tight hand on my shoulder and said, "No, she doesn't understand. We don't have those names. I'm Bett. She's Lizzie."

He laughed. "You can trust me. I'm a friend. So we have first and second daughters here."

"My little sister is finding it not easy to give up her name. But she'll learn. I hope the learning is not too painful for her."

Josiah told us that he lived just outside of Sheffield on the road to Stockbridge and came to work in the mill. He took care of the machines, sharpened the saws and planes, and supervised the cleaning of the place.

"Who are these men?" I asked.

"They are slaves," Josiah said.

"No, the white ones."

"These men were put on ships sailing out of Europe. Some were homeless street wanderers, some were thieves and murderers released from prisons, and some are from insane asylums. When they landed in America, farmers and merchants paid the ships' captains a price of passage and got free labor for a term of four or five years. They're called *term slaves*."

"They don't get much care, do they?" Bett asked.

"No. African slaves are better taken care of because the master owns them for life and at least wants to keep them healthy. Some of the termers, though, are hardy, hard-working people who, soon after their freedom, buy slaves."

He changed the subject and looked Bett in the eye. "I am sure I will see you again. What shall I call you?"

"My name is Bett."

"I'll see you, Bett," he called out to us as we walked on.

Away from the mill were large lots where the master's cattle huddled together to keep warm, their breath giving off puffs of steam. Brom worked among the cattle. "*Hoe gaat, het broertje?* [How are you, little brother?]," we called to Brom.

"*Goed. Hoe gaat het mijn zusje?* [Good. How is my little sister?]" Always glad to see his sisters, he laughed and talked with us in Dutch. Far away from the house, he and Bett also spoke in their language. I understood some words and loved the soft rhythmic sound, but Olubunmi had forbidden my learning. Bett asked Brom about Josiah. He did not know him very well, only that Josiah was well respected, liked among the men.

Brom told us how happy he was not to have to work in the fields or in the mill. As a Fulani, he had not known that kind of labor.

"*Dag! Tot ziens* [Good-bye! See you again]," we said as we left him and walked on through

a field where wheat and flax had grown, that
now lay fallow. We came upon a man working
near the building where our homespun clothes
were made from the sheep's wool.

"Good morning," Bett said. When Bett saw
that he spoke no English, she said "*Goedemor-
gen*." He did not understand her Dutch either.
She then spoke to him in Fulfulde: "*Jam, wurro
waalii?*" Tears of joy rolled down his cheeks
as words rolled off his tongue. As we were leaving him he said, "*Tiigaade!*" Bett answered,
"*Imo jeyi hoore mum!*"

"What did you say to him?" I asked Bett.

"I asked, 'Did your community spend the
night in peace?' That is our way of saying an
early morning greeting."

"And what did he say to you?"

"That he is a Mandinka with the Christian
name Zach Mullen. As we were leaving he said,
'*Tiigaade* — hold on steady.' And I said to him,
'I will hold on to my freedom.' "

Zach had a wide gap between his top front
teeth. "Bett, why are his teeth so far apart?" I
asked.

She laughed and said, "That is his opening to
God."

Happy that we had met a person just arrived

from our homeland, we walked on, close by the dark lazy river that crept through the plain.

It was Bett's duty to arise each morning at four o'clock to have the fires lit in every room of the house by five. The rooms had to be warm by six, or seven, when the mistress and master were called to start their day.

At first I did only small jobs, here and there, but on my seventh birthday, I was told I must now work in the kitchen. I had to bring in the wood for the fire, scour the dishes, sweep the floor, and do anything that Nance wanted me to do. I must be on hand in the kitchen during the preparation of meals and the cleaning up after meals. I also had to heat the water and fill the pitchers in the bedrooms for the morning bowl baths.

In the winter, heavy snow packed itself around windows and doors. We tried to fight it with hot water and salt, but the snow won, and gloomy days seemed to last forever. Working in the warm kitchen was the most wanted work in the house.

In spite of the cold, many visitors came, and we all had extra fires to light, bath bowls to fill, and beds to make; but with all the extra work and the mistress's sharp temper, Nance remained kind and motherly. Still I longed for Olubunmi.

Nance had taught me how to lay a fire so that it would blaze quickly. She showed me how to clean the heavy iron pots that hung over the fire without getting the greasy soot on my clothes. She helped me learn to sweep without scattering the dust. She laughed a lot and told me stories when the mistress was not around. That was not often.

Our master, not a big man, not small either, was even-tempered; most people looked upon him with respect. He was a landowning merchant, who took care of business. Being very rich, he had special foods delivered from afar: chests of lemons and Seville oranges and many kinds of teas. The pantry held dried fruits — apples and pears — canned berries, and crocks of jams and jellies from which to choose. There were fresh apples in the cellar and barrels of cider, Jamaican rum and rum made right on the grounds from molasses.

Nance had a wooden sour tub in which she mixed dough sweetened with molasses, and set it to rise. The loaves, brown and crusty outside, were moist inside. Those loaves could have lasted a good ten days without becoming dry, but Nance baked bread every Thursday. She was a good cook and even though Mistress Anna was stingy, Nance saw to it that Bett and I were well fed most of the time.

Though our mistress had come from a wealthy family, she had an eagle's eye and a miser's hand. Every day she portioned out all the ingredients for the meals that were to be prepared. She kept on her person the keys to every pantry and every cellar door. Rarely did she forget to relock them, but when she did, Nance always took out a little extra that we shared. A little bit, unexpected, brought joy and pleasure all the more warming because it was shared in secret.

There were some things, even though plentiful, we were never given. Pickled pork was one. One day the mistress forgot to lock the pantry that held the crock full of it. That night we did not fall asleep as soon as darkness fell. We savored those bits of meat, and as always during happy moments, I begged Bett to tell me stories we had heard in Claverack. "Tell me about Yaaye," I pleaded, using our word for mother. "Tell me again what she was like."

"What is every yaaye like? Beautiful."

"No, tell me what she was really like?"

"It is late. We must sleep. You will not want to get up in the morning and the mistress will be unhappy."

"Let her be unhappy. I don't like her."

"Don't, Aissa! Never become a prey to those kinds of feelings. Say your prayers and *welterusten* [good night]."

That night I dreamed a beautiful woman held out her arms for me. How I struggled to get close, enfolded, but I could not reach her. When I no longer tried, she came closer and I knew it was Olubunmi. I felt a strange warmth that relaxed me the way riding on Fatou's back once did. Olubunmi said, "*Mijn kindje* [my child, her endearing words for me], you must not be so angry. Life is hard now and will be, but pay attention to your sister and try to be like her."

Bett and I overslept, and when six o'clock came we were still lighting the fires.

"Lizzie! Lizzie!" The mistress's shrill voice rang from the top of the stairs. I heard her but I didn't answer. Nance looked at me and said, "Child, whut's wrong wid you. Go, go, she's callin'."

Mistress Anna was leaning over the bannister

in the stairway, her long hair streaming about her face, red with anger. "*Potverdorie!* [Darn it!] Come up here this moment."

I rushed up the steps.

"Why do you refuse to answer when I call?"

"Meesteres, I don't," I replied, not looking at her. Then I looked up. There was such anger on her face that I backed away. She grabbed me by the shoulders.

"Why do you refuse to answer when I call?"

"I don't always remember that name, Lizzie. I'm Aissa."

The force of her open palm against my face snapped my head around. And a voice inside me said, *Don't cry. Stand and die before you cry.* I straightened my shoulders and looked her in the eye, and she lowered her head.

As I refilled her water pitcher for her morning bath, I wondered, Why? Why was I in this place with this angry woman? But I soon forgot her when it was time to start the day with the first meal.

Breakfast time in the house was the best part of the day. The smell of homemade bread toasting in the warming pan made me feel like being nice. Usually five or six people from far and near sat at the master's breakfast table. Most of the time, Mistress Anna was the only woman.

At first the English food with little spice and seasoning was strange and not very tasty. I missed the food we had in Claverack and was pleased when the mistress showed Nance how to make donkers. How pleasant to have the kitchen smelling of the leftover meats chopped with bread crumbs, apples, and raisins, and sprinkled with savory spices. Made into balls, they were fried and served with boiled pudding. Nance and others in the house, including the master, didn't much care for our donkers, but Bett and I were always happy when the mistress insisted on having them on the table.

4

Sheffield was a busy town. On my many errands, I saw lots of travelers passing through on horse-drawn stages and gigs. There was a lively trade in fur, timber, and live-stock, beef as well as pork. One of the chief trading crops was flax, out of which many women in the town wove their coats and dresses.

The mistress's clothes were brought by boat from far away. Once Bett and I unpacked many cloaks; long trains on gowns of lovely silks and brocade; skirts opened in front and trimmed with stomachers — embroidered triangular pieces that covered the chest and stomach; a bright green silk cloak with a hood; blouses with ruffles at the elbows. She was, indeed, one of the best-dressed women in the town.

During the fall and winter of our first years in Sheffield, the house was always filled with men who owned property in the town. They spent hours drinking and talking in the upstairs room where the master spent much of his time. It was Bett's duty to see that their glasses were filled with ale and their cups with tea, and to empty containers with chewed tobacco and ashes. Brom was taken from the care of cattle to see that the horses and chairs, or gigs, were all cared for properly. Nance was busy in the kitchen preparing scones to serve with tea.

On moonlit nights, guests dropped in unexpectedly. Often the master and mistress joined their friends in sleigh rides and skating parties on the river near the house. The mistress loved to have guests in the drawing room, where they danced until the wee hours of morning or stood talking around the great fireplaces. Bett and Nance didn't seem to mind being there to serve. But I found it boring, the music cold without drums and hand-clapping. We had nothing to do but stand and wait for someone to need something.

Even though we were busy, we still found
time to talk and plan for the two days we were
going to have away from the house at Christmas. On this, our third holiday, we were all
going to Josiah's place, which was in the forest
on the edge of town, on the road to Stockbridge. "Oh, youse gwan have a sho nuf good
time," Nance said. "All de folks from 'round
come bringin' good things tuh eat and music
and song, and dancin' a plen'y."

The week before Christmas the house quieted. Not many guests came, so I let thoughts
about the coming holiday fill all of my days.
And I had never seen my sister so excited. She
asked Nance a thousand times whether there
would be music for dancing. Could Josiah
dance? Did Nance think he would dance with
her?

"What's wid you two?" Nance asked Bett.
"He keep astin' if you comin' and you keep
astin' if he'll dance with yuh. Will yo' brother,
Brom, be speakin' tuh Josiah 'bout bridal business? Will the mistis have uh weddin' on her
hands soon?"

How lucky we were that Christmas Eve was
on Sunday. No one worked hard on that day,
for most of the people, being Christians, spent

much of their time in church or prayer. The master did not insist on our going to service that day. I was so glad. I hated sitting in the cold back gallery with other slaves, away from the stove that heated the place, listening to the preacher tell us how God loved us all, free men and slaves.

Our chores were done early, so we packed all the things for the celebration and set out for Josiah's place early that afternoon. Men and women from other farms joined us and we all walked together. The floor of the forest was dark and cold, and we had been on the trail for a long time when we passed the circular Indian village of the Muhheconnuk people. Their dwellings, made of poles, logs, and bark, were round at the bottom and dome-shaped at the top. White smoke rose from the center of each dwelling and small fires were lit outside. A few men were around the fire in the center of the village. Brom pointed out a tall bronze man as the well-known leader, Miantonomo.

The pale winter moon was bright and cast shadows in the forest as we walked on our way. Some of the men and women who had joined us took turns singing songs they had sung in their villages back home in Africa. We clapped our hands to the songs and made joyful noises in anticipation of the time we would be together, without masters and mistresses.

Josiah lived miles away, but the distance didn't seem far with the talk, the songs, and the cold night spurring us along. Soon we saw torches lighting the way to the little house that sat in a clearing in the forest. The smell of roasting meat filled the air. Then we heard the thump, thump of the drums. Feeling the excitement, I wanted to run on ahead, but I controlled that feeling and kept with the group.

The house was filled with people from the area around and near Sheffield and Great Barrington. Sarah was there. Nance was right. There was not only a great amount of food, but there were many musical instruments: metal castanets, drums, calabash shakers, horns, fiddles, and jugs.

Then the music began. The women danced, Sarah the most lively of them all. Josiah danced round after round with her. Bett stood with me and watched. The women removed their head scarves and threw them at Sarah's feet to invite her to dance.

When only the drummers played, Nance was the first to remove her scarf and throw it at

Bett. Shyly, Bett refused to dance, but others did and I, with the children, clapped while doing little steps on the side. But when the metal castanets and the fiddle and jug players began their music, even the children danced. I danced and danced. By the time the cocks were crowing, I was tired and ready for sleep.

5

The next morning, Christmas Day, I awoke in a room crowded with other women and children. Hastily I slipped over sleeping bodies and found my way outside. The sun was just coming up on the horizon. The air was stinging cold, but already the fires were glowing under a roasting sheep. The men stood about in little huddles, their breaths giving off as much steam as the cups that held the scalding liquid they drank.

I stood alone thinking about Olubunmi and wondering what she was doing this Christmas morning. How I wished she was here with us to tell her stories and to serve her wonderful spiced tea. I wished I was back in Claverack where we knew everyone on the farm and everyone knew us, and where, because there were so many of us, I rarely had to face the master or the mistress. Now it was just Nance, Bett, and me in the house and the few men in the fields and mill. I felt the tears sting my cheeks as they became icy in the cold morning, and I rushed back inside.

Bett was still sleeping, but Nance was just getting herself dressed. "Why you cryin' on dis happy mornin'?"

"I miss Olubunmi."

"Tell me again all 'bout yo' friend."

I dried my tears. "She's a Yoruba woman and knows many things." I told her all about Olubunmi and Claverack, and again I lost control and dissolved into sobs. Quickly, Nance took me outside so that I would not wake the others and ruin their morning with my sadness.

When the sun was high in the sky, more people came to Josiah's. Men stood outside, circled around a fire, talking. The sun crept slowly across the sky and shadows lengthened, but people still came. There was much more food than on the night before, and there were more and better drummers. Everyone was dressed up for the occasion, but with or without colorful outfits everyone was at ease. The laughter and talk were more lively and the drummers more bewitching.

The greatest surprise and the most fun of all was Nance. She was the first to dance. Like Olubunmi, she knew exactly how to excite the drummer, and as she danced I just knew that when she was younger she must have been the best dancer in her village.

Bett had on a hand-dyed cloth wrapped around her body to make a skirt. Her head was tied in a matching blue scarf. Josiah gave her a broad smile and said, "You can no longer pretend shyness and refuse to dance." He was the first to throw a cloth at Bett's feet to invite her to dance.

The drummer beat a rhythm. At first Bett did not pick it up, and everyone groaned. Sarah laughed and said, "The girl can't dance."

Was Sarah jealous because Josiah was attentive to Bett? I knew Bett could dance. She had practiced for this party. So why didn't she show them? I wanted to shout at her, Go on!

"Tain't uh Af'ican woman dat can't dance," Nance said. "Gie her uh beat, drummer."

Bett warmed to the beat and then she and the drummer connected. She danced, her hips and arms one with the rhythm. I'd never seen her dance like that. The drummer beat his drum and everybody became so excited that they all joined in.

From then on, the women threw their head scarves at Bett's feet. She responded to the invitation, immediately connecting and moving with the rhythm. Josiah could not keep his eyes off her. Suddenly, I realized how beautiful my sister really was. She was no longer a girl. She was a woman! Her dark brown skin was clear and her hair was long and very black. Bett was almost six feet tall, well built, and having no problem with her height, she held her shoulders straight and her head high.

Where had she gotten her looks? We were decidedly different. My skin was black and smooth, my hair close to my head. I would probably grow to be no more than five feet seven inches tall. Would I ever equal her in any way?

Being there with all the good food and music, and with Africans like myself, I forgot about the mistress. At midnight of the third day, we started the walk back to the master's house. Josiah asked Bett if he could walk her home. What about Sarah? I wondered. I was not surprised when Bett answered, "Yes."

6

Soon snow turned to rain. The ice melted, Ashley Falls roared, and the streets were a sea of mud. Then one day the birds began to sing, trees to bud, and the tiny leaves quickly grew to hide the nests of the songsters. With the coming of spring, the mistress had Bett put winter clothes away and unpack new, more colorful ones.

Each day grew longer and warmer, and Bett often managed to disappear to collect roots and leaves that Olubunmi said had healing powers. Her trips were a secret from the mistress. Sometimes Bett returned with her hand darkened by stains that were very hard to remove. She was anxious and did not rest until the stains were hardly noticeable. Nance and I often laughed knowing that the mistress didn't see them because she never paid attention to us and assumed that anything dark on us was natural. Bett didn't laugh. She never wanted the mistress to even suspect that she would disobey rules.

The more visits she made to the forest, the more self-assured and independent my sister became. Word was passed along and the men often came to her when they were ill or had wounds that did not easily heal. Slave women came and brought their sick children. I began to fear we could not keep the mistress and master from discovering that Bett's powers were becoming well known.

Once we were out walking when a very thin, distraught slave woman called to Bett. She talked rapidly as if afraid, her eyes fastened on Bett's face. I saw the alarmed look on my sister's face as she said, "No, no. I could never do that sort of thing."

The woman said with anger, "But dey killin' us. You kin save us. Do it."

I could not hear my sister's answer, but the woman turned away with a scornful look, then fled.

"What did she want?" I asked.

"Poison! Something that Olubunmi would never do, and neither would I." She said no more but I knew she was undone.

Josiah came around often. Bett and Brom talked a lot about him, but I only learned of Josiah's intentions to marry Bett when Nance teased her. "Youse glowin', girl. Say yes to de man and be his wife."

"I have nothing to say about that. How can we be man and wife when one is free and the other a slave?"

"Maybe the master'll let 'im buy yo' freedom."

"You think Josiah hasn't asked? The master is willing, but the mistress flatly refuses. She says I was hers before the master married her. She will have the final say."

That night when we were alone, I asked Bett, "Do you want to be Josiah's wife?"

"Oh, yes. I think he will make a good husband and father for our children."

"I'd have a husband but, being a slave, I'd never have children."

"I'm glad Yaaye and Olubunmi never heard you say that. We were taught to believe that to be barren is a very sad thing." A woman who can't have children is like a tree that bears no fruit.

"Well, I believe to give birth to a slave is the worst thing that could happen to me. If children are what you want, then marry. I'm sure Brom will agree." I could not control my displeasure.

"Yes, marry!" she retorted. "The master stands between me and everything that happens in my life. Where we came from, a man who wanted to marry a woman asked her mother. If the woman liked him, then her parents made plans for the many ceremonies. Here the master decides. He is so busy, what is our happiness to him? He wouldn't even talk to Brom."

"Did he talk to Josiah?"

"No. The mistress told Josiah I was not for sale and that she would not give her permission for me to marry. But I'm not worried. Josiah *will* be my husband and I his wife!"

"Ha! You just gave every reason why slaves shouldn't bring children into this world. Why don't we just run away? Live with Olubunmi?"

"Oh, Aissa, Olubunmi is a slave like us. Josiah told me that there are free blacks in a place called Boston, far from here. There, sometimes those free blacks are stolen and sold into slavery. Think of what happens to runaways. Our master is too well known and too rich. He'd get us back and we'd really be in trouble. She'd probably sell you."

"You have powers, Fatou, use them. Make them sick. Kill them."

"Aissa, how dare you! I cringe when strangers think I'd do such a thing, but you — oh, Aissa. The powers given to me are for good. I would never use them for anything else."

"Not even to be free? I'd do anything to be free."

"No. You wouldn't do *anything* even to be free. Would you risk my life? Would you sell me down the river? Think of what you're saying. Please, don't let your thoughts leave you with such a cold heart."

"Then let's run away. Do something."

"That's a great risk. If we had help, yes, but we don't know anybody out there. You must stop dwelling on the *bad* things. We must hold on to the best things we have and not let the mistress destroy that."

"What do we have?"

"We have each other, *Tiiagaade!*" Suddenly she caught herself and switched to English. "Hold on steady and act and behave as though

we *are* free. Then when freedom comes we will
be whole, not sick from hating."

I turned away from her, wondering how she
could say those things. Surely she must have
known that the master and mistress cared nothing for us. How could she care whether I hated
them or not? I lay in the dark listening to Bett
breathing. Soon she was asleep, while I wished
for sleep to come.

7

After the master became a justice in the common court of pleas he was often away, and when he was at home, people who had problems came to the house to talk to him and to get his help. I'd never seen so many strange-looking people. Mostly poor. They had problems with landowners making them pay high rents just to farm the land. The master took time to talk to them, but the mistress looked at them in a way that made most of them twist their hats in their hands and leave the room to wait in the yard until the master called them.

During this time of year the men on the place were always busy calving and lambing. After our morning chores, Bett and I were sent into the fields to help prepare the soil for planting. We worked several hours hoeing and raking, then went back to the house to help prepare meals for the workers who had been hired to do the planting.

On Monday mornings we built a fire under the iron pot in which we boiled the bedclothes, work clothes, and linen. Then we put them in a pounding barrel and pounded them with sticks until all the dirt was out. When they were finally clean, we took them down to the stream and rinsed them. Even with Bett's strong arms to help, it took a lot out of me to get the wringing done.

At sundown, when our work was finished, I ached all over. My hands burned with blisters from the hoe and rake, my back was stiff, my legs sore. I knew Bett was tired and aching, too, for we fell asleep right away without talking. In spite of the hard work, I liked being outside. In a deeply blue sky, sun-filled, snow white clouds floated. Ever-welcome birds flitted about giving their music without being asked, and the wind, being contrary, scattered our piles of straw at the end of rows. The spring air was warm and soothing.

On days when it rained we stayed inside

cleaning lamp chimneys and fireplaces and mopping floors — all the chores that had been left undone while we worked in the fields. It rained often, cold drizzling rain that filled the streams and soaked the earth. One night we huddled together, frightened by slithering lightning and sharp blasts of thunder. There was a loud knock on the door. The master was away for a few days, so we didn't answer. Then a voice called, "Bett, wake up." It was Nance.

Bett finally opened the door. There were two women with Nance, both soaking wet. The eldest said, "You must please come. My daughter is in labor for two days now. Our midwife can't bring the baby. She said you can help if you'll come."

"Where is the mother?" Bett asked.

"Near Great Barrington."

"As far as that? How will we get there in the storm?"

"We have a horse and chair."

"But it is late. My mistress does not allow me to do this kind of work."

"And my daughter will die if you don't."

I looked at the women and remembered them from the party. The daughter had been there, too, her belly round like a calabash bowl.

She was very thin and looked tired and weary then. I wanted to shout at Bett, Forget the mistress. Go! But I said nothing.

"Please," the woman said.

Bett decided to go. I wanted to go with her, but Nance said no, firmly. She and I could hide Bett's whereabouts and maybe the mistress would never know.

It was still raining and cool enough for lighted fires in some of the rooms. With the rain, and the master being away, the mistress ordered her breakfast in bed. Nance decided to serve her favorite breakfast of fruit, warm bread and butter, broiled fresh fish, and tea with cream.

After all this time, the mistress, too, was pregnant and happily expecting her baby in July, several months away. She slept late, went for long walks, and often went for long rides on her favorite horse. Her friends and the master disapproved of the riding and warned her that it could hurt the baby, but the mistress paid them no mind. She made many demands during the day and sometimes in the night.

One could hardly tell that a baby was coming for the mistress had always been plump, with broad hips like the ladies in a painting on her bedroom wall that she proudly said was a work

of a Dutch master. She also had a round face
with rosy lips and cheeks. Her light hair, piled
high on her head, often escaped in little wisps
that fell around her face, giving her a soft look.
Bett said she was pretty, but somehow I always
brought out the worst in her, which was not at
all pretty to me.

At ten o'clock the mistress had not come
downstairs and Bett had not returned. Twelve
o'clock came and the mistress was sleeping. At
two o'clock, wearing a large, soft wrap over a
warm nightgown, she came into the kitchen
with her long hair down. "Nance," she said
yawning, "I'm starving."

"Oh, Mistis Anna, Ah'll give yuh uh good
lunch. Why don' cha go back upstairs and wait?"

"It's cold today and the kitchen is warm, in-
viting. Where is Bett? I would like for her to
do my hair."

I dared not speak. I looked at Nance. Nance
seemed to take forever to answer.

"I sent her tuh git fresh milk. She oughta be
back heah in a li'l while."

"You should not send Bett out in the rain.
Lizzie could have gone." She turned to me.
"Why didn't you go?"

"I was scrubbing the hearth and scouring pans."

Nance, busy preparing lunch, was silent, and the ever-present tension between the mistress and me forced the mistress back upstairs. She had her lunch there and we were left alone. If only the rain would let up. Maybe she would go for a walk or visit a friend. But no. Around three o'clock, Bett still had not returned. We were worried. What if the mistress called for her again? But worse, what if something had happened to Bett?

Just as we heard the mistress stirring upstairs, Bett walked in the back door with a bouquet of lovely spring flowers. Nance rushed to her. "What took yuh so long?"

"The gods chose not to breathe life into the little one. And we almost lost the mother. I could not leave right away."

Bett was hardly out of her cloak when the mistress entered the kitchen. "Bett, where have you been?"

"To gather your favorite flowers to cheer you up in this bad weather." Smiling, Bett gave the mistress the flowers.

"Lizzie." The mistress turned to me. "You

see how thoughtful Bett is. Kindness goes a long way. After dinner, Bett, you can do my hair."

I was in bed when Bett finally came from the mistress. I knew she was exhausted, so I pretended to be asleep. Without getting undressed, Bett lay down next to me and I felt her shake as silent sobs racked her body.

8

The spring rains turned to summer thunderstorms, and the heat became almost unbearable. Many of the whites came down with yellow fever. For some unknown reason, few slaves were affected by the dreaded disease, so we were busy attending the sick, burying the dead, and keeping things going.

Bett, especially, was kept very busy preparing teas. She had learned from Olubunmi to cleanse the body with sweats and baths, and to cool it with dampened leaves. Many people were afraid of baths and open windows, but Bett insisted, and some who listened were cured. Our mistress and master were lucky that they did not get even a light case.

However, during the height of the epidemic,

the last week in July, the mistress complained of nagging back pains. Low-hanging dark clouds had blanketed the place for days and rain had fallen heavily the night before. The roads were mud holes when the master went for the doctor. Bett, knowing how busy the doctors were, said, "I just hope things don't happen here without a doctor."

It was pouring rain. I knew that the master should have been back long ago. Bett, still worried said, "If the doctor isn't here soon, that baby could be in danger."

We stood outside the bedroom door, listening. There were groaning sounds but no call for help. So we went back down the stairs to wait for the master. He finally came back alone. The doctor was away treating fever patients in outlying areas. Other doctors who were much farther away were not available either.

The master was as pale as a sheet and his eyes were wide with fear. He rushed up the stairs without taking off his rain cloak and muddy boots. He must have told his wife the news, for she let out a scream that made Bett, Nance, and me come close together. We did not move when the master rushed down the stairs.

"Bett, I am told that you have proven your-self a good midwife. We will need your help."

"Master, I don't know. The mistress must say," Bett said. "Take me to her."

When my sister returned to the kitchen she told us that the mistress screamed, "Why is she here? Get her out of this room."

The master said, "Anna, dear, Bett can help."

"Whut did she say to dat?" Nance asked.

"She began laughing and said, 'A black conjurer-woman delivering my baby, never! The doctor will come. We'll wait.' "

"She might wait, but dat baby won't wait," Nance said.

The day passed and the master was alone with his wife. We could hear screams through the closed door. Bett paced up and down, up and down.

"Would yuh hep her if she called yuh now, after whut she done said?" Nance asked.

"Yes!" Bett answered quickly.

"If you put yo' foot in dat room and she done waited too long and die, yuh know you'll be blamed. Dey'll hang you."

"I'm a healer, meant to save lives; if I'm asked, I'll help."

We had dinner ready for the master, but he didn't appear. Bett went up the stairs to see if we were free to leave. We were not free to go to our rooms until the master said so. We waited. The doctor didn't come. We lit the lamps. It was hot and the humidity made us uncomfortable, but we fanned ourselves and waited.

I had fallen asleep on the floor near the cellar pantry when I was aroused by the master's heavy footsteps on the stairs. He looked so alarmed I was sure the mistress was dead. "Confound that baby," he said. "It's killing my Anna." He went back up the stairs.

There was silence. It seemed as if no one dared breathe. The sound of rain and croaking frogs, which I had often found soothing, now was a discordant din. Then the master called, "Bett, come quickly."

Nance and I sat in the kitchen waiting. It was late and we had not eaten because the master and mistress had not had their share. Surely that baby would come soon. We huddled together waiting for something to happen, dreading to know what it was. We waited. I went and lay on the floor. In spite of my dread and fear, or maybe because of it, I slept again.

Nance shook me awake as the master was

calling, "Come see. We have a fine boy up here."

Nance and I rushed up the stairs. The mistress was drenched with sweat and as white as the sheets on her bed. She looked weak and worn, but when I came into the room, she mustered enough strength to demand, "Get that wretched devil out of here."

Later, Bett told me that finally the baby, John Ashley, came. The third male in that family with the name John. Bett said that by the time John was born, Mistress Anna was holding onto her, pleading for any help that Bett could give. But when she had her baby at her breast, she thanked her husband for saving their lives. The master thanked Bett, and from that day on, my sister did not need the mistress as a go-between. She went directly to the master and was heard.

9

Years had passed. More children had come: Jane, Mary, and finally Hannah. Little John grew into a fine young man who was popular in the town. He was invited to the many picnics along the water and to skating parties and sleigh rides. He, like his father, was well dressed in knee breeches fastened with silver buckles over black silk stockings, and with buckles a bit bigger on his shoes. John looked nothing like either of his parents. He had a high forehead, blue eyes, and a straight nose. Every morning his long hair was carefully braided, in what he called a queue, and rewound around his whole head. And small curls that had remained in paper until he finished breakfast were let to fall on each side of his neck.

John was known as the baby Bett had delivered, so Bett's fame as midwife and healer had spread throughout the area, and not only among slaves. As her fame grew, the master gave her more responsibilities. Bett answered the door and decided who would see the master on business that pertained to the court.

The mistress was not pleased with these additional duties and often tried to interfere when Bett had made a decision. One day the house was quiet and not many people had come all day. In the early afternoon, a young girl with her hair uncombed, her clothes wrinkled and dirty, knocked on the door.

When Bett brought her in, I was surprised to see someone so young. Her dirty face was streaked with tears and her gray eyes with long black lashes showed that she was afraid.

"Why are you here?" Bett asked.

"I must see the judge," the child said in a timid voice.

"Sit down and I will tell the judge you're here. I know he'll see you."

When the mistress came into the kitchen and saw the child, she became red in the face. Her eyes flashing, she asked Bett, "What does that baggage want?"

"To speak to the master."

"What does she want to say to your master?"

"I don't know, ma'am."

"I know." She turned to the child. "You slut, you're here because you tempt honest men. Get out of my house. Out!"

I had never before seen my sister lose her patience with the mistress. "You sit right there!" she said to the child.

Mistress flew into a rage. "This is my house and she will go, and she'll go now."

The child, frightened, rose to go. Bett stepped between them and said to the child, "Sit still." She turned to the mistress. "If this child has a complaint, she has the right to see the judge; that's lawful." The child saw the judge.

It was not long afterward that the master gave his permission for Josiah and Bett to get married. The mistress went into her room and stayed for a few days. She tried to alienate young John from Bett, but that didn't work. I sometimes felt that John thought Bett was his mama, instead of the mistress.

Women who owned slaves usually gave the bride a wedding that was celebrated in the yard. Not Mistress Anna. Bett's wedding was planned with the help of Nance and, of course, our brother, Brom. Everybody was invited to Josiah's house for the occasion. I was more worried than excited about Bett getting married. What would happen to me when she went to live with Josiah? Would the mistress let me live with them?

The night before the wedding, Bett was very sad. I thought she was tired, for she had picked fruit all day and helped to prepare it for canning.

We lay in the darkness and the silence was so complete that I knew something was wrong. "Fatou," I said. I had not called her by that name in a long time, and she burst into tears.

"What is it? Do you no longer love Josiah or want to be his wife?"

"Don't be silly. Of course I want to be his wife. If only Yaaye was here. She would tell me what to do."

"What is there to do that Nance, Brom, and I can't do?"

"Where our parents came from, a marriage took a long time to arrange and settle. A wedding was not done in one day. It was a big occasion. There was the dowry from the man's parents, announcing the engagement, signing the wedding contract, and other ceremonies.

Families on both sides were together in all of that."

"Josiah talked to Brom and they are planning you a wedding."

"That's nothing. We have no family. There will be no drinking from the calabash, no dowry, no really big feasts. And there's no one my age to talk to, to share my doubts and my joys." She burst into tears again.

I went to her and took her in my arms. "Please. Don't. Why are you crying like this?"

"All the women in Claverack said an African girl was usually married at fifteen or before she was twenty. Here I am older and don't know how to care for a husband. If I was home, my family would give me their blessings and I would go to Josiah ready to make him a good wife."

If only Olubunmi was here, I thought. She would know. I didn't know what to say. The only married woman I had ever known was the mistress. Suddenly I understood why my sister was crying.

10

That Sunday afternoon in September 1770, the autumn sun was bright on leaves that were just beginning to change their green cloak for one of many colors. Even the weather favored Bett on her day. The women had saved their rations of sugar to make cakes and the men had fished and hunted for fowl and venison. I had joined other young girls and boys to pick berries, apples, and wild greens. The drummers came early to warm their drums by the special fire that had been built for that purpose.

The excitement spread throughout the house and into the yard. Brom strutted about being important, for he was presenting his sister to a bridegroom. He was dressed in the regular homespun pants, but he wore a vest woven from flax that had been bleached white. I was pleased with my brother and proud of the way he was making sure that Bett's marriage would go well. But I was still uneasy about what was going to happen to me.

Just after the master, without his wife or Hannah, their youngest, arrived with the other children, it was time for the ceremony to begin. The drummers beat their drums and all of Josiah's men friends formed a procession and came out of the house into the yard carrying gifts. Then Bett's women friends came with gifts. Of all the people there, I knew of only one African who could read and write — Josiah. He then produced a paper and read it aloud. "I, Josiah Freeman, before my friends, state my intentions to marry Bett who is part of the Ashley house. I have no family. She has no family. So I ask her brother, Brom, to take this contract and give me her hand."

Brom took the paper and went inside and came back with Bett. She was wearing the black skirt and white blouse that had belonged to our mother. The colorful scarf in which she had carried me on her back was tied about her waist and hips. Nance had tied a bright cloth on her head. She walked just behind Brom with her eyes down, looking not like the Bett who lately had been in control. But when Brom placed her hand in Josiah's, she stood tall and the cloth on her head made her look regal. Brom placed an X for his signature and Bett placed an X for hers, and the contract was signed. Everybody cheered. She was now Bett Freeman.

Josiah's friends invited everyone to eat. There was so much food: venison, quail, and mutton. The table overflowed with apples, berries, cakes, and vegetables from Josiah's garden and the wild greens that were to be found in many places. The master, John, Jane, and Mary shared the food. Soon afterward they left. I was glad that Hannah and her mother had not come. The two were very much alike.

I was so excited I couldn't eat. And I was also still worried. What would happen to me when Bett was not there to remind the mistress that kindness goes a long way? The drummers and musicians were playing and people were dancing and I was still not free of my fear. Bett came to me and said, "*Mijn zusje,* why are you not happy for me?"

"I am happy for you. I'm scared. What will happen to me? Will Mistress let me live with you?"

"Mistress will not let me live out here with my husband. I will be there every day. On Saturdays maybe I will leave when my work is done and return on Mondays in time to begin my day. You'll be fine. Now eat and have a good time. This is my wedding day."

Everyone was singing and clapping their hands when considerable excitement burst forth as a medium-height, muscular, very black man came into the yard. He hugged Nance, and out of respect for the elderly said, "Yaaye, how good to see you."

"Grippy, how yuh ever git heah from so far?" she said as she hugged him to her bosom.

"By boat, by chair, but mostly by foot. But seeing you and my friend, Josiah, in the midst of this celebration makes it worth every mile walked. My friend" — he turned to Josiah — "introduce me to the bride."

"Who is he?" I asked Nance.

"Agrippa Hull, a free man. His ma and pa wuz free. He works fuh a man who cares li'l for the po', less for slaves, but gies Agrippa respec' 'long wid pay."

The men were laughing at the jokes Agrippa immediately began to tell. "Yes, we went to hear Lemuel Haynes, this fine educated minister, at the church . . ."

"Who is 'we,' Grippy?" one of them asked.

"My boss and I. Now, you know Lemuel is a mulatto. When it was all over, the boss asked, 'Well, how'd you like the *nigger* preaching?' I said, 'Sir, he was half black and half white; I liked my half, how did you like yours?'" Everybody laughed.

"What's happening out there in the world?" With that question we all became quiet and attentive.

"Some old, some new. The king's men are really getting more riled up with these people around here not wanting to pay their taxes."

"There are some angry farmers around here, too," Josiah said.

Grippy said, "In Boston, March fifth of this year, about fifty or sixty men, most of them sailors, were led by this brother of ours, Crispus Attucks, from Dock Square to the British garrison in King Street."

"Against the king?" one of the men asked.

"You could call it that," Grippy answered. "They protested when the British attacked a young lad. The British fired on them, killing five. Crispus was the first to fall. Things have been boiling ever since. I'll not be surprised if the Colonials go to war."

The questions and the conversation became more and more lively, the men arguing back and forth about the possibility of freedom and on whose side they would fight if there was a war.

"I'd fight for the king against the masters," Brom said.

"Fight for the king?" Josiah asked.

"If the king would free me, then I'd surely fight for him!" I said. The silence frightened me and Bett grabbed me by my arm and pulled me from the group.

"How dare you speak when men are talking. Women are seen, not heard."

I was embarrassed and angry at Bett, but I felt some satisfaction when Agrippa said, "I wager the king's men will offer freedom for your service long before the Colonials do." He walked away from the group to get some food.

The wedding celebration went on and on with dancing, singing, hand clapping, and feet stamping. The sun was long gone from the red horizon when Nance, Bett, and I entered the master's house.

11

The first winter of sharing Bett was not easy, but I soon became accustomed to spending Saturday nights and Sundays alone. My bed without her was cold and I missed the comfort of her voice and her silence. At first I could not sleep. Every sound seemed to be just outside my door, and the rustle of the wind in the trees, which once made me grateful to be inside, now made me want to leave the room and find a more secure place. How glad I was when Monday finally came, and the routine in the mistress's house and in our little room began again.

Snow and ice hampered travel, but there were still those who braved the weather to visit the master and carry on the talk in the upstairs room. After having listened to Grippy and the men, and thinking about the possibility of freedom, I was now more interested in what Bett had to report.

One evening she rushed in late. "There is a newcomer in the meetings, a Master Sedgwick. He's a big man with a pleasant face. I think he is a bit showy, but the men have all taken to him. They are now writing on paper things that they are 'resolved' to do. That word 'resolved' is said again and again. Oh, Aissa, if only I could read! They throw away a lot of words on paper that I'd like to read and learn what this is all about. Maybe I could understand the words they use, like *entitled, liberties,* and *privileges.*"

Night after night, Bett brought more exciting news about the men's talk she heard in the upstairs room. When she finally finished serving the guests and came to bed, she wanted to tell me what had happened. I was so sleepy most of the time, but I listened. I was often disappointed when the talk got underway, for it said little about us and our being free. But she was so excited that I forced my eyes and ears open to please her. Bett went on.

"There was one thing Sedgwick said that I will never forget. I said it over and over in my mind to remember it: '*We in the state of nature are equal, free and independent of each other, and have a right to the enjoyment of life, liberty, and property.*' Aissa, you hear that?"

"I'm listening, but what does that mean?"

"That means we should belong only to ourselves, not to the master, not the king, to nobody."

"We belong to nobody. We have nobody to belong to," I said.

"We belong to Master Ashley. Why do you always act as if you don't know that we were born on Master Hogeboom's place where Baaba and Yaaye were slaves and that we were slaves sold to Master Ashley?" I could tell when she was upset. She used baaba for father and yaaye for mother.

"I belong to nobody."

"It's too bad that you never heard Baaba tell us many times how he became a captive."

"I don't think I would have liked hearing that."

"It's something you should know, and I'm going to tell you. When Baaba was a young boy, there were wars and slave raids. His village was burned and many people were killed. Those who lived were taken to the village of their enemy. One day, some white men came with guns and gunpowder, and Baaba and others were traded for those things.

"They were blindfolded and made to walk many miles until they came to a building, right on the seashore, made of rocks and stones. The men were crowded into small rooms with chains and shackles on their legs and feet. Women and children were put in a courtyard near the ship's captain and his men. It was hot and dark, for there were no windows and no light from the sun. They were fed two times a day and not allowed to move about until night.

"Those who talked the same language were separated. They were kept in this place for weeks, and more captives were crowded in with them. One day three hundred and thirty-nine of them were lined up and washed down and sprinkled with lime dust. Then a small door opened onto the sea. The light from the sun blinded Baaba and for a long time he could not see what was happening. When his sight returned he saw the ship, *Friendship Brig.*

"First the men were put on board, then the women and children. When Baaba finally passed through the small door down into the ship, he had no idea it was the 'door of no return.' Never

again would he hear the sounds of the night
that he so loved: the animals calling their mates,
the drums with their messages of war and peace,
dancing feet and songs.

"For days, too many to count, they were
shackled deep in the hold of the ship. In the
darkness people around him groaned their misery in a language that he could not understand.
The groans and stench made him sick. But the
sickness, as bad as it was, did not compare to
his fear and loneliness.

"He recalled all the stories, all the myths that
might give him some hint of this horrible fate.
There were no gods to appease, no magic to
summon to end this suffering. Was he doomed
to die like those around him, two or three in
the night, far from home, out of the memory
of ancestors, family, and friends, his spirit not
properly released, his bones to lie in a liquid
grave at sea?"

"Stop! I don't want to hear it," I cried.

"You must. What will you tell your children
when they ask about Baaba?"

"I will never tell them that he was a slave."

"You will. Just like he told us, again and
again. So you listen. Finally, they were on land
again. Barbados. Green lush land with palm

trees, breadfruit, and golden pear, what we call avocado. But it was not home and the journey was not over. He was separated from those who arrived with him, their numbers having been greatly reduced. Now there were only two hundred and fourteen of them.

"He was sold to a trader. For days he slept in an open shed where each morning he and others were placed on the block for sale. In the afternoons he lay under the bright sun, his eyes always on the sea eastward, his thoughts of home as he regained his strength eating papaya, oranges, and mangoes, and drinking the cool milk of the coconut. In the light of day he lived wondering what would happen to him in this new land; at night in his dreams he was always back in Africa.

"When he was not readily sold, the slave merchant used him to translate the languages of the slaves to determine from where the slaves had come. There in Barbados he saw many Africans, but only a few who spoke his language. And when he heard his language, his heart leaped in his chest, but afraid that he would never hear it again, he stayed a distance from the one who spoke it until they could disguise their kinship.

"He grew into young manhood. Not very tall,

he had smooth black skin like polished ebony
and his hair was tightly curled to his head. When
Cornelis Hogeboom purchased him, he also
bought ten other slaves. Our mother was one
of those ten."

"Fatou, tell me now. What was she like?" I
pleaded.

"Baaba says when he first saw her, he knew
she was different from other women. Beautiful,
bold and shy at the same time. She was tall, the
color of chocolate, and she wore her long hair
in one large braid with a thin strip of cloth tied
at the end. When he asked her name, he was
surprised at her almost defiant answer, 'The
name is Ayisha.' She spoke in Fulfulde, con-
firming his belief that she was a Fulani. He, of
the Mande group, had long associated with the
Fulani, so he spoke her language, too."

So that's who Fatou looks like, I thought, and
I remembered her dancing at the first Christmas
party and at her wedding. I look more like our
father.

"The journey ended in Claverack, the wil-
derness that was called New Amsterdam. Baaba
at first thought he would have to work for
Hogeboom only for a while, show his abilities,
and soon be able to do things for himself, get

married and become part of the people, the way
slaves were treated in Africa. He wanted to own
a small plot of land. But after ten years he saw
that he was not ever going to become part of
the life of Claverack. He became moody, didn't
do his work. Once he ran away and stayed in
the woods for two whole weeks. He had no
place to go, so one day he came back to the
farm, dirty, hungry, and very tired. The master,
thinking that Baaba had escaped or died, was
so glad to have his property back that he did
not punish Baaba.

"Soon after that the master gave Yaaye to
Baaba in marriage. Over time they had seven
children, including five sons. Again, Baaba
thought surely his children would be given a
chance to grow to be part of the people of the
town, but no. No people from Africa, even
those who were not bonded or bought, were
treated with respect. He knew then that he was
in a strange land that did not know him, would
never know him, because he was not wanted to
be known.

"With the slaves increasing on the farm, our
brothers were sold for money, and the highest
prices were paid by southern plantation owners.
Baaba showed his rage. That was when he was

beaten to death. Yaaye gave up. Lost in her memories and grief, she died. We were sold to Master John and Mistress Anna, so we belong to them."

I lay in the dark thinking about Baaba and Yaaye and the words that I hardly understood: free, equal, and independent. But deep down inside of me I knew. I belonged to nobody — no master and no king.

12

The roads passing through our town were now widened and in fair condition, so many people came through. Some stayed, and the population of Sheffield increased.

Bett remained a loyal slave, but she also continued her duties as a wife, midwife, and healer. Any money she earned for her outside work went to the master. When paid with old clothes, chickens, a goat, or a sheep, those she was allowed to keep.

As time went by, I learned to adjust to Bett's being away much of her free time. She stayed on the plot of land she and Josiah owned, on which they kept the animals and planted a garden. Sometimes, late on long summer days,

Bett and I would go to her small house. There were only two rooms — one where people gathered and a tiny room where she and Josiah slept. The kitchen was separate from the house, with a stone oven and an open fire over which cooking pots were hung.

I loved being with them and often went to help them after Bett and I had worked all day at the master's. Working in Bett's garden didn't seem like work at all. As we planted and weeded, we laughed and sang, Josiah's voice ringing clear and beautiful. And when we weren't singing, Bett talked about what was going on upstairs. She told Josiah of the talk about separation from England.

He was interested and excited and wanted to hear all about it. "Are they saying why they want this separation?"

"Every one of them there is rich, and they're riled up about a lot of things."

"Who are some of them?" Josiah asked.

"Deacon Smith, Captain Fellows, Dr. Barnard, and Dr. Kellog, and recently, a lawyer named Sedgwick."

"They're the rich rich," Josiah said, and we laughed. "I would guess that most of them don't want out from under the king."

"I'm not sure about that. Some are determined to take themselves from under him,"
Bett said.

"I think most are not," Josiah said. "They may
be angry all right, but what will they do about
farmers who rent from them? If they don't want
to pay taxes to the king, farmers will not want
to pay taxes to them."

To my surprise, Josiah spoke as if he knew
what was going on.

Bett said, "That's what Deacon Smith
brought up. Farmers will think they should have
as much as the rich men have and will cause
trouble. But Master Ashley said they shouldn't
worry about poor farmers, but about New
Yorkers who want to claim the Massachusetts
territory."

"Did the others agree?" Josiah asked.

"Lawyer Sedgwick said, 'Yes, men without
property have no say in what will happen. What
we say in this room refers to those of us who
own the land, not to those who are renters and
laborers. We must rid ourselves of the king and
the Dutch who want to claim that New York's
eastern line is the Connecticut River.' "

"I'll bet Master Ashley didn't go along with
all of that," Josiah said.

"He agreed that although the New York Dutch were the first to find the Connecticut River and trade with the Indians, that gave them no claim to Massachusetts. But he didn't agree about the king."

"I knew it. He's a staunch Tory," Josiah said.

"What's a Tory?" I asked.

"I didn't think you were listening, Aissa," Josiah said affectionately. "That's a person who is loyal to Britain and wants no part of independence."

Bett went on as though we had not interrupted. "Oh, there was a lot of loud talk then. The men taking sides. Master Ashley reminded them that if they refused to pay taxes, things could get worse. That they would be no match for the king's soldiers. He said, 'Do you want war?' Deacon Smith and Dr. Barnard agreed with Master Ashley."

"What about the others?" Josiah asked.

"They were with Master Sedgwick. And by the time he finished using those words freedom and liberty, everyone agreed that they should send the king's men packing. Master Ashley kept quiet. And the writing went on."

I listened to them talk while we planted pumpkins, potatoes, all kinds of squash, spinach, and a small plot of wheat. When the moon was full, we often talked and worked until it was time for us to walk back to the master's house.

Then I noticed that Bett was sleeping more than usual. She was often sick in the mornings, was short-tempered, and didn't want to get out of bed. I was worried. One morning, I was so alarmed I ran for Nance. "Come, come, I think Bett is poisoned."

Nance rushed to our room without getting dressed. "Whut you been eatin'?" Nance wanted to know.

Bett laughed. "My poison will be over in nine months. Rejoice, I am going to have a baby."

Bett's sickness did not last long and soon she was growing round, her stomach like a calabash. She went about her duties pleased and happy with herself. Josiah appeared pleased, but also very concerned. One night I heard him talking to Bett.

"We were not wise in conceiving this child. Because you are a slave, he, too, will be a slave."

"How do you know it's a he?" Bett said, trying to lighten the conversation.

"Please, this is serious."

"Who knows how serious more than I? I'm the slave. But I want a child. I have hope that slavery will end and she will be free."

"Don't say 'she.' We will have a son. I will work hard and buy his freedom. You will see. There is no law that says a free man cannot buy his child."

Not long after that, Agrippa came to town and Josiah invited African men, free and slave, to his house to greet him and hear what he had to say. Agrippa had heard about Colonials wanting to petition the king for independence, but not about the petition being written upstairs in the Ashley house. Josiah called Bett into the room and asked her to tell what she had discussed with him.

Bett, heavy with her unborn, was shy and reluctant. I knew her shyness was not due to her pregnancy alone. "She's not going to talk," I said. "She believes that, among men, women should be seen and not heard."

They all looked at me as if in disbelief. Agrippa said, "Bett is a good example of an African woman who knows her role as wife and mother. You would do well to watch your sister and become like her."

There were those words again. I was determined not to be like Bett. "Maybe. But Bett is the only one who knows anything, and if *she* doesn't talk, then you'll know nothing."

They all looked at Josiah as if to ask, You have a woman in your house who is as disrespectful as that? Josiah surprised me. He seemed disappointed with Bett, not me; and I think he was a little ashamed that a woman who knew so much was made unwilling to share. He urged his wife to speak, and she became the center of attention when she told about the writing of the document and the plan for freedom and self-rule in the petition to the king. She repeated those words that headed the document: *"We in a state of nature are equal, free and independent of each other, and have a right to the enjoyment of life, liberty, and property."*

There was much excitement and the men there asked many questions. "Wuz us Af'icans spoke of at all in dis talk 'bout freedom?" Zach wanted to know.

"When will the county hear about this?" Brom asked.

Bett didn't know when, and she answered, "We were never mentioned at all, and what mention they made of the farmers and poor was that they were to be under the rule of the rich, as the rich were under the king."

"They speak of life, liberty, and property. Those of us who are not free are 'property,' " Agrippa said. "Men like your boss, Josiah, and mine are not interested in ridding themselves of their 'property.' "

"They are only interested in getting more. But we must keep our eyes open. Bett will be our ears and when the time comes we will be there to speak our minds, too." Josiah spoke calmly.

After that meeting, for a while Josiah was not as warm toward me. Was there something wrong? If so, why didn't he say so? Then finally he said, "Aissa, I wish when you are in the discussions of men, you would hold your tongue. We have a saying: *The hen knows it is morning, but she watches the mouth of the cock.*"

"She waits for the cock to crow, right?"

"As she should."

"But why?"

"It is an African custom and our customs keep our people safe."

"But Josiah, we are here and women work just as hard, side by side with the men. And we are treated just as harshly. So why can't we speak for freedom, too?"

There was silence between us. In his calm manner, he finally said, "Because we are here under these unusual conditions, it is all the more important that our customs survive. And I hope you will remember that."

I didn't agree, but I said nothing, knowing that whenever I had the opportunity to speak out for *my* freedom, I would speak.

13

On December 1, 1772, Bett, with Nance and with my help, delivered a fine baby girl. I had thought Josiah would not be happy with a girl. But he was very pleased. Proudly he held his baby and, showing her to the north, south, east, and west corners of the earth, he said, "I name you Ayisha for your grandmother, Omosupe [oh-MOH-soo-peh] because a child is the most precious thing, and Freeman because your father is a free man."

When the master registered the child as his slave, Bett said, "Her name is the same as mine: Bett." The master was pleased.

With Bett being so busy, Little Bett became as much my baby as hers. I tied her on my back and felt her warmth and her little heartbeat, and for the first time I loved, expecting nothing in return.

In January of 1773, there was much coming and going in the Ashley house. The plan that my sister had talked about became the Sheffield Declaration. It was now ready. Josiah called his friends and others together and Bett reported, "Master Ashley and his friends are planning a town meeting for all the citizens to hear what they have decided to send to the king's representative. The master still seems uncertain about separating from the king, but certain that he wants the Bay Colony of Massachusetts to draw the borderline between them and New York."

"That John Ashley is a Tory, isn't he?" Agrippa said. "One of a few around here who fully supports the king. He must know that a lot of people don't care for him because of that."

"Things are changing and he is beginning to see he has to be either for this colony or for the king. I think he is for this colony," Josiah said.

"It doesn't matter who they're for, I want to know who's for *us?*" Brom said. "We have a right to freedom and liberty just as much as they have."

"Agrippa, as free men we should go and see what this is all about," Josiah said.

"Why don't you take 'resolves' like theirs and present them?" Bett asked.

"To the king's representative?" Agrippa asked.

"No, to Master Ashley and the men who wrote *their* declaration," Bett said. "Add your words to theirs."

"Bett is right. We must be ready with just what we want to say," Josiah said.

All that Saturday night and the next day, they worked on the paper, Bett remembering much of what had been said in the room upstairs. Agrippa did the writing. I was so proud of all of them — the men and Bett working together. My hopes of freedom filled me with joy. I looked at Little Bett, finally walking on her own. I lifted her up, hugged her close, and whispered into her ear, *"Mijn schatje* [my honey], we'll be free, free, free!"

On January 12, cold winds were blowing and the icy rain was in heavy clouds just waiting to drench those many white men and few free blacks who had come from around the county to accept or reject the Sheffield Declaration. Bett was as nervous and as anxious as any of the men who had done the writing. I knew if she had been a man she would have been there at the Sheffield town hall, but *no* woman, slave or free, was allowed to attend.

Around noon rain was still falling and the cold winds were even more cold. Finally, after waiting for the master a long time, lunch was served, and I was busy finishing the cleaning. As if she had suddenly gotten the idea, the mistress said, "Lizzie, I want you to go to that meeting place and take your master some food and hot rum."

In that icy rain, I thought. Hot rum would be cold by the time I arrived. My body tightened with anger, but I said nothing as I wrapped myself in an old shawl that would do little to protect me from the rain. Nance wrapped the food and drink in thick layers of cloth, tied to give me a handle.

Along the muddy road, horses still hitched to wagons stood heads down, their bodies giving off steam. I hurried, the icy rain stinging my face, numbing my hands. When I came to the hall, just beyond the tailor shop, I went toward the front, but the crowd there was so thick I was afraid that I would not be able to enter. At the back the crowd was just as thick.

Knowing that I had to find the master, I forced my way inside. The heat, the stench of damp bodies, and the fog of tobacco smoke gave me a fit of coughing.

Moving beyond elbows and rough coats, I soon found the master up front seated on a small platform with about six other men, all of whom I had seen in the house. I recognized Lawyer Sedgwick, a broad-shouldered man with a big body and large head, who was reading aloud from a paper. A white scarf around his neck accented the pink face that stood out even more because his hair was thinning. His voice was deep and loud enough to be heard throughout the hall.

On seeing me, the master frowned. When I held up the bundle, he smiled and waved me forward. "The mistress sent this," I said. He opened the bundle right away and drank from the jar of rum, which was still warm. I sat in back of the platform listening while I waited for the master to finish. When Lawyer Sedgwick completed the page, someone in the back shouted, "Lawyer Sedgwick, I didn't understand all that you read. Please read it again."

"Yes! Yes!" came shouts from around the room.

One of the men on the platform stood. "We must get on with this business."

Lawyer Sedgwick said, "I will read it only once more. There must be order if you are to hear."

The hall became quieter as he read. "Resolved that Mankind in a state of nature are equal, free and independent of each other and have a right to the undisturbed enjoyment of their lives, their liberty and property."

I am in this meeting, the only woman. I am here! I thought. I became so excited but also afraid that they would notice and ask me to leave. I pulled the shawl around me and tried to pretend that I was not at all interested in what was being said.

"Resolved that the great end of political society is to secure in a more effectual manner those rights and privileges wherewith God and nature have made us free." He read on, a lot of things I did not understand nor have any interest in. The master placed the plate and the jar on the floor and covered them over, but he gave no sign that I should leave.

When the reading was finished, Lawyer Sedgwick asked that a vote be taken and that the town clerk record the proceedings. Then, to my great amazement, Josiah and Agrippa forced their way to the front of the room. Josiah was dressed in his usual attire, leather breeches and leather shirt with fringes at the yoke and at the hem, but Agrippa wore a coat flared at the bottom. A red scarf at his neck partially covered a white shirt with ruffles down the front. His black velvet trousers had buckles at the knees. The two, though differently dressed, were imposing figures. There was a rustle in the crowd and then quiet, as if everyone was waiting for a great happening.

My heart beat wildly while Josiah stood beside Agrippa, both of them calm and composed. Agrippa's voice rang deep, clear as a bell. "Gentlemen. You say that 'mankind in a state of nature are equal, free and independent of each other, and have a right to the undisturbed enjoyment of their lives, their liberty and property.' What does that mean to the five thousand slaves in this colony? We petition you."

Then he read from the paper they had drafted: *"For, in as much as you claim to be acting on the principles of equity and justice, we cannot but expect you to take our deplorable case into serious consideration and give us ample relief which as men we have a natural right to. We are desirous that you have instructions relative to our cause in your petition and pray that you communicate our desires to the representative of this colony. In behalf of our enslaved brothers and sisters, in this province and by order of their committee. Signed: Agrippa Hull and Josiah Freeman."*

There was stirring and angry grumbling in the room, and then scattered applause, but Lawyer Sedgwick quickly silenced the hall. "Your petition should have been presented at the time of the writing of this declaration," he shouted.

"But honorable sir," Agrippa called out, "we had no knowledge that such a petition was being prepared."

There were more rumbles through the crowd. Lawyer Sedgwick reacted quickly to gain control. "We cannot now recognize such a petition. I call for the vote."

Before more could be said the process was under way. Showing no signs of defeat, Josiah and Agrippa made their way to the back of the room. How could they remain so calm? I was raging inside. Was it because I was a slave? I grabbed the dishes, wrapped them carelessly, and escaped from the hall as quickly as I could.

It was still raining, the streets hardly passable because of the mud. But I didn't hurry. When

I arrived, I was soaking wet. The mistress was waiting. I knew she was angry, but no more than I for different reasons. "Where have you been so long?" she shouted.

"Mistress, I waited until the master had finished to make sure he wanted nothing more. He was busy and took his food as he had time." I stood and looked her in the eye, waiting for her response.

"Your after-lunch chores are waiting for you. Do them right away."

"I am wet from the rain, mistress."

"Do your chores right away."

Josiah visited us that evening. Bett wanted more details from him of what had happened. He told her and ended by saying, "We warned you. Africans and wives are property. They are not ready yet to place your rights over property rights."

Bett, with her everlasting hope, did not appear upset, but I burst into tears, still feeling the hurt and pent-up anger. Josiah put his arms around me and said, "In due time. Don't be so impatient under the yoke. As we learn our rights and our duties we will understand that we are not meant to be slaves. When we understand this, we will free ourselves."

"I know now I'm not meant to be a slave," I cried. "Help me! Tell me what to do and I'll free myself, now."

Josiah and Bett looked at each other. I saw the tears in her eyes as they both quickly left the room.

14

We had just celebrated Christmas and a New Year when Bett came in talking about a lot of tea being dumped into the Boston harbor. Upstairs they called it the Boston Tea Party. "They emptied all the British East India Company's tea in the sea. All of it."

"Who?"

"Some say the Indians. But upstairs they say it was colonists who dressed up like Indians on a dark night and destroyed that valuable tea."

"Why do they dress like Indians?"

"They're cowards and want the soldiers to think the Indians did it so they can be killed."

"The mistress complains all the time about

how much tea costs. Why would they throw it
into the water?"

"*Because* it costs so much. And now the king
has put even more tax on it, and closed off the
harbor until they pay for what they threw into
the sea. We can't get tea, sugar, nothing from
other places."

"Oh, I hate to think of what the mistress is
going to do. She'll be hard to live with now."

At Christmas in 1774, things were rough in
our town. We had some sugar and molasses but
no tea. Everyone was angry and on edge, not
knowing what was going to happen. I would
have missed the sugar and molasses, but not
their tea. Bett knew how to make the best tea
from her roots and leaves, teas that the mistress
would not have dared to taste. So she suffered.
The children missed the puddings, tarts, and
pies, but things got worse before they got better
and our holiday was spent without the usual
fun.

One morning a messenger came to the door
with a sealed packet for the master. Bett led
him upstairs. Later she gave him some hot
scones and cheese. The message was for Mistress Anna, all the way from New York, and

even before the messenger had gone we knew that the news was not good.

Our old master, the mistress's father, Cornelis Hogeboom, then a sheriff in Columbia County, New York, had been killed in an anti-rent squabble. He had gone to settle a dispute between landowners and renters who claimed that they had paid the landlords and the landlords' children more rent for the land than the land was worth. They were determined not to pay more. "We are paying rent under a system here," the renters declared, "that was overthrown in England in the thirteenth century."

Sheriff Hogeboom had gone to a land auction that had been put off again and again and was further postponed because of the argument. As he started to leave, a shot was fired in the air. Some men, dressed and painted like Indians, suddenly appeared and followed the sheriff and his men. They fired more shots. His men ran, but the sheriff refused to spur his horse because he was a representative of the law and didn't want to appear a coward. The men dressed like Indians soon left, but one named Arnold, the leader of the anti-renters, chased the sheriff and shot him in the heart.

Mistress Anna fainted when she was told that her father's last words as he fell from his horse were, "I am a dead man." We were all upset and actually sorry for her. She wanted to go home, even though the journey was difficult and the funeral would have long been over by the time she arrived. Still she cried for the master please to let her go.

The master grieved, too. But he knew that the border wars between Massachusetts and New York and between landlords and renters were dangerous and that the trip was long and hard. He did not want to risk taking the children on such a journey.

About three months later, Bett showed another messenger into the master's upstairs room. When she came down she told us, "The master is so sorry that he did not go with the mistress to Claverack. Her mother is dead from grief over Sheriff Hogeboom."

The mistress put all of her beautiful clothes away and dressed in black. Her face became thin; streaks of gray began to show in her hair. She moved like a ghost in the house that was still bustling with visitors coming and going to the meetings that were held upstairs. Besides that hustle and bustle, the children were lively and had lots of friends who were in and out of the house. It was Bett's duty to take them to parties and pick the girls up from music lessons and John up from tutoring, and to see that they got to water picnics.

Of the four children, I liked Mary, the oldest girl, the best. She had a sense of fairness and could see through the rage and tantrums of her mother. Knowing this, her mother ignored Mary, giving much undeserved attention to Hannah, who was so like herself — demanding, impatient, and often cruel to her sisters. I was also her target. Hannah delighted in telling her mother things about me that caused the mistress to go into rages.

One day I came in from the field to find Hannah in the middle of the kitchen floor with mud from her head to her toes. She started screaming and the mistress came running into the room wanting to know what had happened.

"She put me in the water and made me sit there," Hannah said, pointing at me. With her eyes tightly closed, her little mouth opened with earsplitting screams. The mistress grabbed a green stick and began beating me over the head and arms. Mary cried to her mother that I had not been there. Hannah had played in the mud after being warned not to. With this distraction, I was able to escape back into the field.

Later Mary came to me and said, "Lizzie, I'm sorry. Hannah is a liar."

"It's not for you to be sorry, you're just a child." Then I remembered she was her mother's child and said, "Thank you, Mary. You are a good girl." She clung to me, her small arms around my waist, and I began to understand how my sister could let go and feel for some of them. Without the mistress knowing, Mary and I became friends.

The talk of freedom among the slaves and free Africans did not stop. Josiah and Agrippa continued to petition the governing body. Then one Saturday night when we were at Bett's house, Agrippa came with three other free Africans from around the colony: Peter Salem, Felix Holbrook, and Salem Poor. I could tell these were not men from Sheffield. The fire in their eyes and in their voices let me know they were different.

They had heard about the Sheffield Document and about the declaration that began it. Sheffield could become the first place to free slaves. "But are these honest men?" Peter

Salem asked. "Do they believe these words, or are they just mouthing them?"

"Their words are far-reaching," Josiah said, "not only for African slaves, but for slaves from England and other countries. When I look about, I fear they give these words with one hand and take them back with the other."

"We must have faith that they believe them, not only for themselves, but for all men," Grippy said.

"We will find out only if we petition them as we have others. Our chances here are better because they have made the declaration. So let us send our petition," Salem Poor said.

Of course, my sister was all for it and very excited. She and I listened as they argued back and forth before they came up with a petition that stated: *". . . Your petitioners . . . have in common with all other men a natural right to our freedoms without being deprived of them by our fellow men as we are a freeborn people and have never forfeited this blessing by any compact or agreement whatever."*

They talked awhile about being brought here and enslaved, how bitter our lives were and how husbands and wives lived as strangers. Finally, I said, "What about the children? What about us who live all of our lives without hope of ever being free?"

There was that ominous silence that always followed my questions or statements in the company of men. Bett's head shot up, and her back stiffened with indignation. I waited.

Josiah looked at me and smiled. "That is my sister, Aissa, who insists on being heard. I guess in this strange land where we often work equally hard and are treated equally harsh, she feels that the demands for freedom should be made by women as well as by men."

"Aissa," Agrippa said, "we'll consider the children."

To my surprise, these words were added: "... *If there was any law to hold us in bondage ... there never was any to enslave our children for life when born in a free country. We therefore beg your excellency and honors will ... cause an act ... to be passed that may obtain our natural right our freedoms and our children be set at liberty at the year of twenty-one.*"

15

We were very happy and filled with hope when on February 25, 1774, a "warrant" calling for the annual town meeting was issued containing the following issue number: "101y, to take into consideration the present inhuman practice of enslaving our fellow creatures, the natives of Africa." Our hopes were dimmed when the item was put off for a few weeks for study.

In the meantime, one morning Bett and I were doing chores in and around the room where the mistress and master were still at the breakfast table. He was reading the paper that came maybe three or four times a year. "John, dear," the mistress asked, "tell me what is all this whining about slavery? All I hear is talk about freeing slaves."

"It's nothing for you to worry about," he answered matter-of-factly.

"It's part of our investment, so it *is* something for us to worry about. What would happen if we freed the darkies? How could they take care of themselves? They're like children and they're lazy, stupid, raucous, and loud."

Potverdorie! And right in front of us as if we were pieces of furniture! I looked at my sister. Her face was as if cast in stone. I waited for the master to bring the mistress to her senses. For a while he acted as though he had not heard. Then he said, "You're right. I would feel sorry for them if they were free, on their own."

I started laughing. "Sorry for us to be free?" I said through fits of laughter. Bett looked at me, frightened, as if I had suddenly lost my mind, but I couldn't stop laughing, knowing that my laughter, out of place, from a joyless feeling, must have branded me insane.

The master quickly got up from the table, grabbed me by my shoulders, shook me violently, and then slapped my face. "Take her out of here," he said firmly without raising his voice.

For the rest of the day there was silence between me and my sister. That night Bett spoke first. "I wish you hadn't heard that this morning. I could have exploded, too, but I try hard not to give them the pleasure of knowing they break my heart."

I didn't want to talk about it. I tried to remain calm. "What if they did free us, Bett?" I asked. "I would go to Boston where all the free blacks are and live a good life."

"What do you know about Boston? Don't listen to Grippy. He's a man and can roam around. You're a woman and need the protection of a master or a husband."

"Then I'll have a husband."

"Oh, so you want to get married? Who would want you for a wife, *mijn kindje?*" Bett teased.

"I can cook, clean, sew, and work at anything that needs to be done. When I'm free, I'll be so happy."

"I sometimes think that maybe things might not be well for us when we're on our own. We could become like those white women paying off a debt. You see how hard they work and how badly they're treated."

I looked at my sister and I had no idea from where I got the thoughts that came into my head. "I don't understand you, Bett. Have you forgotten those women only have to work for four or five years and they'll be free? I'd work hard, too, and not mind, if I knew that one day I'd be out from under the mistress. I'm a slave forever with no hope of being free."

I waited for her to answer. She said nothing.

I went on, "Could our lives be any more miserable if we were free? Don't you wish you could go and live with your husband and not be depending on the mistress or master to tell you what to do? We know how to work. Suppose you could keep your money? You could have nice things for you and Little Bett. You have nothing but leftovers. Can't do a thing unless the master or mistress says so. Slavery is misery."

"That's the difference between me and you, Lizzie. I spend my time counting my blessings."

"*Potverdorie!* Don't call me Lizzie. I'm Aissa!"

"You call me Bett and I don't shout at you."

"You like that name, always did. But I can't believe you like this life."

"This life will change," Bett said firmly.

I, too, wanted to believe that this time they would look at the words they'd written, see us as human, and set us free. With a feeling of hope, I waited.

On March 14 another meeting was called. The majority voted to delay action, the subject "being under the consideration of the general court." Bett was happy that at last our freedom was in the courts. She had faith.

"What is the court?" I asked.

"The place where they decide by law."

"Who?"

"The master and others."

"Why can't they decide now? The people here voted it."

"Don't be so impatient."

My anger overflowed and I lashed out, "You and your patience. What does it get you? You work night and day to fill the master's pockets; you do everything to please the mistress and give all your attention to her children, leaving me to care for Little Bett. And right in front of us they talk as if we are cats and dogs in the house. I'm not like you, thank goodness! I have no patience for slavery and no love for the master and mistress. I hate the mistress; I hate the master; I hate being a slave."

"Mark my word! Go on hating and it will turn

on you, and the one you hate most will be your-self," Bett said.

Pay attention to your sister. It was as if Olu-bunmi's voice were in the room. I trembled with fear and anger. I didn't want to be like my sister. I didn't want to know my place as a slave. I only wanted to know my place as free.

16

Sheffield was among the first counties to have a meeting on ending slavery and on declaring in favor of independence from the king. The general court acting on the will of the people agreed that there should be an end to slavery and sent the bill to Governor Gage to have the king turn their wish into law.

This time the mistress, feeling threatened, pleaded with the master to send a petition to the governor to forward to the king, asking that the wishes of ruffians and backwoodsmen not be heeded. Men of property did not wish this to happen. It was those who had nothing and wanted nothing that wished to destroy the colonies and the king's rule.

Acting on instructions from England, Gage

refused to sign the bill. The slave issue died. But the town became divided between those loyal to King George III and those who wanted independence and self-rule. Bett brought rumors about war between farmers in the backwoods, the Indians, and the king's men. No one knew if or when war would come to Sheffield.

That spring, 1775, Bett and I had to work in the fields most of the time, for extra help was hard to find. Men were leaving the area to muster — gather for roll call, march, and learn the methods of war. For this they were paid more than for field work. Word came that the king's men had sent out their soldiers to capture guns stored at a place called Concord. Then there was fighting in another town, Lexington. The people, riled, began to fight the king's men in Boston. A real war had begun.

Right away, the rich men in Sheffield pledged their support to the people of Lexington and began to raise an army. No longer were the secrets kept in the upstairs room. Everyone was talking about the Colonials forming a Constitutional Congress that would make the laws for the colonies, and the colonies would become united states.

There were many town hall meetings, and on

June 18, 1776, all the white Colonials in and around Sheffield came together. The poor pledged their lives, the rich their fortunes to secure independence for Massachusetts. They voted to support the Constitutional Congress if that body declared the colonies independent of the king. On July 4 of that same year the colonies declared themselves independent of the king.

In early August, when the news came to Sheffield, a holiday was declared. People shouted, slapped backs, and finally organized a parade with fifes and drums. I had never seen so many people so excited. Caught up in this fevered fun, Little Bett and I, too, marched in the parade. By the time we reached the town hall, hundreds of people were already there, including free blacks and slaves. Little Bett and I stood with the other slaves; my sister stood with the mistress and the mistress's children.

The master stood with other men of wealth and property on a platform that had been hastily built just outside the hall. The crowd waited in a festive mood. Finally, the town crier quieted the people with his strong voice and began to read. I was surprised that, even to the back of the crowd, his voice rang clear:

"When in the course of human events, it becomes necessary for one people to dissolve the political bands which connected them with another, and to assume among the powers of the earth, the separate and equal station to which the Laws of Nature and of Nature's God entitle them, a decent respect to the opinions of mankind requires that they should declare the causes which impel them to the separation."

He paused and then waved the paper in the air. "This document will tell why we as a mature people must break ties with the mother country, become independent, and explain our reason to the world. It begins with a declaration of rights:

We hold these truths to be self-evident, that all men are created equal, that they are endowed by their Creator with certain unalienable rights, that among these are life, liberty and the pursuit of happiness. That to secure these rights, governments are instituted among men, deriving their just powers from the consent of the governed."

I listened, waiting to see if he would explain what all this meant. Where were we in *this* paper? He read a long bill of indictment of the king that was often stopped with applause. And finally:

". . . these United Colonies are, and of right ought to be Free and Independent States; that they are absolved from all allegiance to the British Crown, and that all political connection between them and the State of Great Britain, is and ought to be totally dissolved; and that as free and independent States, they have full power to levy war, conclude peace . . . and to do all other acts and things which independent States may of right do. . . . And for the support of this Declaration, with a firm reliance on the protection of Divine Providence, we mutually pledge to each other our lives, our fortunes and our sacred honor."

The crowd exploded with shouts and applause. I looked at the people beside me, wildly expressing their happiness and hope. Over the noise I asked, "What does it all mean?"

"It means what it says," one of the men answered.

"Does that 'men' mean black men, and all women, too? And that liberty, does it mean we'll be free and protected?"

"Well — "

"Can we, too, own property? And that happiness? . . . I doubt they're talking about us."

"Aw, Aissa," someone said, "why do you always cloud things with your questions? Have faith. It's got to mean us, too."

17

Josiah came to the master's door asking for my sister. I ran to get her. Rarely did he come unless it was something mighty special.

"I came to tell you that they need soldiers so badly that a deacon in the church wants me to go to muster, learn war, in place of his son," Josiah said. "He'll pay well, enough for me to buy little Ayisha. Plus, if I'm let into the big army I'll get twenty pounds and one hundred acres of land."

"No, no, I don't want you to go," Bett said. "You could be killed."

Josiah. Killed. Is that why the deacon didn't want his son to go? Oh, no. What would life be without Josiah? He made us laugh; the joy he brought Little Bett, all of us, could never be replaced.

"I know it's dangerous, but with that money I can buy the baby, you, and Aissa."

"How dangerous is it?" I asked.

"Too dangerous to risk for our freedom," Bett said. "It is not only his being killed. It is also his killing. Once it's over, even if he lives he will be dead."

"What do you know about war?" Josiah asked, his voice raised.

"I know. I saw the killing of the Indians and the white men when I was just a child. But I remember."

"It would take me forever to raise the money I can get by going to war. My mind is set on it." He held her in his arms and kissed her long. Then he hugged me and kissed me on the forehead. Little Bett clung to him as if she understood. Then he said good-bye.

A few days later, Josiah returned. His shoulders were bent, and his face was more stern and his smile no longer there. "They refused to let me substitute for the deacon's son. I was told that there is no place for a black man in the ranks of what is now being called the Continental Army." He was silent for a moment as we stood in disbelief. Finally he said, with little enthusiasm, "I hear the British are taking us."

"Then go fight for the British," I said.

"But what if they lose? I got property here. Not much, but still land that's mine. And I know this place. Where will I go if they lose? I like the words spoken here about freedom and liberty. Men who believe that will, I feel, stand by their words and do justice by all men, black and white, rich and poor."

I could tell that Bett felt both relief and outrage. Relief that he had returned and outrage that a man as courageous as her husband was denied the right to make a choice.

Upstairs they were discussing what to do about the war and what to tell the people in the next town meeting. Bett was moving in and out and heard much of what was said. She walked about for days with her back stiff, her head high. She seemed sad and not excited as she had once been about what they were saying. I had to prod and plead with her to talk.

"I thought it was just the mistress and the master, but the others, too, speak things about slaves right in front of me as if I'm not there. Do they not see me at all? Their mighty General Washington will not have Africans in his army for fear the British will think our own men are not willing to fight. And some of them say the British are poking fun at them for having Africans fighting with them."

"But Josiah says the British are taking blacks. So how can they poke fun?"

"The British probably think they are pretending to be better than what they are. Saying they love liberty and freedom while still holding slaves. Not a one in that room dares to admit that. They say we are stupid, untrustworthy, lazy, unable to fight. You should hear them."

So that's why she has been so sad, so stiff-backed. She was suffering under the urge to lower her head to a bleeding heart. Was she losing faith in the master's lofty words? I wondered. She went on talking.

"There's only one, who has not been here before — Tapping Reeve, a lawyer who heads a law school in Litchfield, Connecticut — who admits that white men don't want to fight and the war is being lost. Aissa, there are five hundred thousand of us in this land. He said that. And that we could be the ones who affect the way this thing is going, depending on which side takes us in first. He's afraid it's going to be the British."

I didn't know much but I said, "If the British will give us our freedom, let's pray they win."

"Who do you think owns us? Mostly British! Think of what my husband told us. Who decided that we should be slaves when the people wanted to end it? The king and his governor. And what if the king loses and we've cast our lot with him? Where would we go? They say the British have only forty-two thousand soldiers. The Colonials have nine times that many."

"I don't believe it. With that many men, how can they be losing?"

"The Colonials will only stay three months in the army and then they go home. It takes more than three months to make a good soldier." Bett went on talking about what they were planning to do, but I was not listening. I was thinking about what would happen to us after this war. Were the British really giving slaves freedom? How could Africans choose between these two? I wanted to believe that somewhere there was somebody who knew that slavery was wrong and how much we wanted to be free. Maybe it was the British.

18

In January 1777, everybody was talking about the war. Thousands of slaves were joining the Redcoats, the name the Colonials had given the British because their uniforms were red coats with white shirts and trousers. And the British were winning. The new Congress decided to draft men for service. Even though everybody said Britain was winning, most of the newly formed states still didn't send in their quota of men. In June of that year, a town meeting was called in the name of the government and the people of Massachusetts.

Josiah was there. He told us a committee, which included Theodore Sedgwick, was picked to set up plans to draft men for the Continental Army. At that meeting they voted to add a bonus to that given by the government to men drafted from their state. However, they did not make plans to draft Africans, slave or free.

Bett was happy to have Josiah with her when many of the women whom she often saw in the town complained that their men were away at war. She knew that they envied her not only for having Josiah around but also for being fairly well fed, clothed, and in a decent house. And she carried herself in such a way that they never knew that she was a slave owning nothing, not even her own life.

Her happiness did not last long. Things became so bad with the Continental Army, Massachusetts was asked to contribute fifteen battalions. The men upstairs said that, with 67,000 men in the state at that time, they would comply. This did not include slaves. Those efforts didn't count for much. Battles were still being won by the British. The capitol in Pennsylvania fell, and in December of 1777 General Varnum asked for permission to organize a battalion of slaves.

I remember the day word came. We had not celebrated a good Christmas since the Boston Tea Party and were looking forward to a small get-together on that New Year's Day. Just three days before the new year, word came that some slaves and free Africans were being recruited in Sheffield. This upset Bett very much. She heard the master telling his friends that black men would never be treated as equals in battle. If they were captured they could not be exchanged as equal prisoners of war. Never would the British exchange a white soldier for a black one.

"What will they do with the blacks?" one of his friends asked.

"Sell them to plantation owners in Barbados."

"Is that true?"

The master laughed. "Whether it's true or not, it will make many a one of them think twice before trying to get freedom through the army. They are paying owners for their slaves, but I'll not let one of mine go at any price."

All slaves knew that to be sold off to Barbados and to southern plantation owners was a fate worse than death. Bett was determined that Josiah would not hear of the recruitment. However, Josiah did hear and told Bett he was going. Alarmed, she told him what the master had said.

"Do you want to be shipped off to Barbados?"

"I hope you don't believe everything you hear upstairs in that house. I hear things, too. The British aren't afraid of us. They have many of us fighting on their side. It's your master who is worried about what will happen to him if slaves are armed. And what will happen if slaves left behind get ideas about freedom. I can earn twenty pounds and gain one hundred acres of land if I join that battalion. Massachusetts will give me a bonus of another twenty pounds. I'm going."

Bett said nothing. She helped him pack an extra coat, two warm shirts, homespun under-clothes, and a pair of leather trousers.

Many of the slaves and free Africans gathered to say good-bye. Just as he was leaving, Bett gave him a warm blanket that she had been given for the last child she delivered. She and Little Bett walked with him down the road. I wanted so badly to go that last mile, but I knew they needed those moments together, alone.

Word spread that Zach Mullen, along with some men from other farms, had gone off to fight for the British who promised them free-dom. One day Zach showed up, saying he had been sent back when his officer found out that he was from the Ashleys' place. The master threatened to beat him.

I was working in the field the day Zach returned. The field supervisor sent for the master. What would happen to Zach? I wondered. I was so afraid that the master would whip him within an inch of his life. Pretending to go about my work as usual, I was doing more listening.

"Didn't you know you wouldn't get far?" the master asked. "I should give you the whipping of your life." He fingered the whip that he held in his hand.

Zach stood with his head up, his hands clenched in fists behind his back. He breathed heavily in the silence, not moving his eyes from the master's face.

"Go to work," the master finally said.

Why had the master backed down? Could he have been afraid Zach would run away and try fighting with the Colonials and Indians? Was Zach ready to take on the master? Maybe the master was just glad he had his slave back.

When Josiah had been gone for a while and the war was still being lost, Brom went to the master and asked to be sold to the slave battalion. A fair price was being offered, as high as four hundred pounds. The master had paid only forty for Brom. The master told Brom he was worth far more than four hundred pounds to him. There was a shortage of men to tend cattle and work flax. He was needed here to help win the war.

Brom told me he asked, "But will I be free when the war is over?"

The master answered, "Only if you become a soldier in the army is freedom guaranteed."

For days Brom moved around like a man with no reason to live. He talked about running away to join the British. Zach warned him against that. He had learned the hard way. Ashley's place was too well known and the British wanted to have friends in the area whether they won or lost.

Brom did not try to join the British. He refused to eat. He drank little water, but Bett forced him to drink her tea. Still he grew thinner and thinner and looked terrible. Bett and I pleaded with him to come to his senses and not kill himself. One day Bett said to him, "Have you forgotten Olubunmi and her wisdom? She always told us, in our heart and soul, to say yes to living; say no to bondage and nobody can keep you a slave. Brom, *tiigaade!*"

Little by little he got better. Maybe he understood something Olubunmi and my sister, too, fully understood that I was still unable to grasp.

Several months went by. We heard no word from Josiah. Bett lost weight. She did not sleep well, and the work on her place suffered. Little Bett missed her daddy and kept asking when he would come home. We had no idea whether he had been able to find his way to General Varnum's line to join the slave battalion. We waited.

One evening, the sun was red on the horizon. The first star of the evening hung low in the sky. We were still working in the field when Little John came running, waving a letter. He was out of breath. "It's from Josiah."

Bett was so excited, I think she didn't realize, as she hurriedly opened the letter, that she couldn't read. She hugged the pages as the tears rolled down her cheeks.

"Here, let me read it for you," Little John said.

"Not here. I must prepare myself. I must sit down." He hadn't been in our quarters since he was a small boy. Now, as a young man, he seemed out of place sitting on the floor. Bett sat in our one chair, I on the bed. We listened as Josiah's voice rolled over us.

Bett, Dear Wife:

I have been in Newport, Rhode Island, for about three days now, waiting to leave here for Pennsylvania. This state is in ruins. Their rich dairy farms are destroyed; the source of their wealth, the trade in slaves, thanks goodness, is totally wiped out. The British blockade is complete.

There are many Africans here. I have been fortunate to meet a few. One is a Miss Obour Tanner. At her home I met a well-known woman who writes poetry that has been read by many, here and abroad. Her name is Phillis Wheatley. She read some of her poems. I was thrilled, for it made clear why we must join in this fight against what she called tyranny. You would love her, a beautiful person with a gift one can hardly believe.

They still don't want us to be allowed to fight. I think the owners of slaves are willing to lose the war rather than part with their property. But, as a free man, I have been signed up and should join General Varnum in his all-black battalion before long.

So far I am well, but I can see that war is not good for the mind. I now understand your not wanting me to go. But remember, I will be home

and take you away from there to one hundred acres
of our land, and we will begin a new life with
Ayisha and Aissa.
    God be with you and ours until I see you again.
                    Your husband, Josiah Freeman.

When John had finished reading the letter,
he carefully folded it and handed it to Bett and
quietly left.

"The mistress will hear about this. Will you
let her read your letter?" I asked.

"The mistress is never out of your mind, is
she? Why would she want to read my letter?"

"Why does she want to own us? Will you let
her read it?"

"No."

I took the letter and pushed it in between
planks in the wall so that it could not be seen.
"You can't read, so what reason is there to keep
a letter?"

The next few days we went about our work
with a sense of relief, knowing Josiah was now
with the army. With Little Bett now seven years
old and in the kitchen helping Nance and doing
the chores that were once mine, I spent more
time in the fields. Late evenings we worked at
Bett's place and planted crops there. Little Bett
was calm, an even-tempered child like her

mother, and did not often raise the mistress's ire.

Early one morning as we were about to go to the master's field, the mistress summoned Bett. I went ahead. The sun was already giving a warning of a hot day. My long dress was not at all comfortable in this work. I often thought how nice it would be if we could wear pants. Men had everything made easier for them. If I were a man, I thought, I'd be in Boston where the ships come and go. Far away from this place — gone to where Baaba and Yaaye came from.

I had not seen Bett until she was right upon me. I knew she was angry and upset. "Now what?" I asked.

"John told about the letter. The mistress said she'd waited for me to come and tell her, or the master, about it. Why hadn't I come?"

"Why did John tell?"

"He had to. I don't blame John. I knew he'd tell. And I told her that with John's telling, there was no need for me."

"Was she angry?"

"She's always angry. She demanded to see the letter. I told her I didn't have it. She ranted and raged and said I had better get it and bring it to her or I would be severely punished. Then, Aissa, I remembered what you'd said. 'I can't read,' I said, 'so why would I keep a letter?' She called me a liar and said she would find it. 'Get to the field!' she shouted. So I'm here."

I was frightened for Bett. What would the mistress do? I wondered.

That night when we went to our room, we found it in shambles. The mattress was off the bed, covers scattered all about. Our belongings were all over the room. Bett's herbs were spilled, all mixed together. I had never known feelings of such humiliation and shame. I looked at Bett and for the first time our eyes could not hold. We both lowered our heads. I was surprised that of all the feelings that rushed over me, anger was not one. Helplessness and anger do not go together.

We did not speak but we both went to the wall. The letter was still there. We burst out laughing. We laughed until tears rolled down our cheeks. In our defeat we had won.

19

The mistress punished Bett. She would not let her away from the place day or night. With all the leaves and roots of the herbs mixed together, there was no medicine for Bett to use, and being watched so closely, she could not go into the forest to collect what she needed. Although the mistress was angry, and refused to let Bett see others, she still had Bett do the most personal things: comb her hair, help her dress for her outings, and serve her meals when she ate alone.

It was Bett's duty to go through the mistress's clothes to find what needed mending or restyling. Mistress Anna Ashley gave away few clothes. Of course, neither Bett, Nance, nor I could wear her things. Sarah could, and often

Sarah was called to do the mending and restyling for a small fee and a worn garment.

We had not seen Sarah for a long time. With the shortages of men and of food and other supplies, we had few get-togethers on our rare days off. There had been no Christmas parties, and the one day off for the New Year had been spent on the place. So when Sarah came to sew for the mistress, we were all very happy to see her.

When Josiah chose Bett for his wife, Sarah was jealous. But soon after Sarah was married, her feelings of jealousy had disappeared. She became a friend again. We were all having breakfast together the morning she arrived. Brom greeted her politely, but the rest of us shouted and laughed, hugged her, and set a place for her at the table.

We felt lucky to have someone bring us news from the free Africans in the area. Sarah told us that many of the men had gone to war, many for the British. Bett told Sarah about the letter from Josiah and seemed proud that he had decided to fight on the side of the Colonials. When Sarah heard that the mistress had destroyed all of Bett's herbs, she told us about an Indian woman who might be willing to share some that she had.

"How will I get to her? I can't go anywhere. Not even to my house and farm."

"Oh, you would have to go. She would have to see you and talk with you to be sure you were the right person. Not just anybody is trusted with their medicines."

"The invisible spirits will find uh way tuh wing you dere," Nance said. "Will it, and de way'll be dere."

Bett, Brom, and I went with the others to the field, leaving Nance and Little Bett to their house chores and Sarah to her sewing. We sang along the way passing the cobble, the rocks that seemed all the more white under the blue skies. Ashley Falls roared in the valley, which was carpeted with flowers in bloom.

We worked on the far end of the farm near the dense forest. With the shortage of men, there was no one to supervise our work. Sometimes the master appeared late in the day and sometimes Little John might ride through with his friends to see how things were going. Suddenly, I had an idea. "Bett, why don't you go and gather herbs?"

"You know I can't do that."

"How will the mistress know? Who's there to tell? We'll do enough work so that you'll not be missed."

In the middle of the day we took little time to eat our bread and berries and to drink from the pail, for we wanted to make sure we did Bett's work and ours. When the darkness from the forest spread outward and made shadows on the hills, my sister returned. She carried a bark basket on her head with one hand and in the other she held her head scarf tied around leaves and roots.

"How did you ever gather so many in such a short time?" I asked.

"You'll not believe this. The forest was so peaceful that my mind didn't stray from my purpose. My eyes saw everything clearly, and I was busy digging when suddenly right upon me was this tall bronze man as straight as a strong young spruce. He wore white leather pants and shirt and a band of beads around his head. Strangely, I had no fear and I smiled at him and said, 'The peace here is still undisturbed.'

"He knows Josiah and was pleased to hear I'm his wife. Then, as if out of nowhere, this woman appears. She, too, is tall and straight as an arrow. Her wrinkled skin, brown as a walnut, and her round black eyes marked her as one with wisdom. Immediately, I thought of Olubunmi."

Suddenly my chest and throat filled with the tears that would not flow, and I was glad that my sister did not notice as she went on with her story.

"She spoke her native tongue to her son and he asked me who was I and why was I in the forest. I told her my name and to whom I belong. I assured them I was alone. That I was there to gather herbs for healing. She asked questions of me through her son. What was I looking for? How did I use it? She always smiled when her son responded. Where had I learned? I told her all about Olubunmi and how she had taught me all I know."

"Did she show you anything new?"

From the bark basket Bett took a yellow-brown rooted plant with hollow stems that held about fourteen leaflets with sawlike notches along the edges. The rose-colored flowers were small, close together in a flat-topped cluster. The fragrance? I could not describe how wonderful.

"She told me how to use it, but her son had

no way to tell me the name in our language. Then she helped me gather all of the things I needed to replace my supply. That's why I was able to get so much in such a short time."

I looked at the well-made basket and knew it was a gift from one healer to another, and I felt a bit ashamed that I had not given the right respect to my sister.

Finally the mistress forgot about the letter, and Bett and I were able to go to the farm. We had expected the place to be overgrown, the animals to be either dead or lost, but to our surprise, things were not as bad as we had thought they would be.

We found the goats in the woods, the chickens thinner but in place, and the weeds not unbearable. So, in time, things were back to normal. If only the master would grant us just *one* day to work for ourselves.

20

The war kept the master and his friends busy with planning and scheming how to get more men for the Continental Army. Bett, again, found herself always rushing between her regular chores and keeping the master's company satisfied in the upstairs room. Not only did they deal with the demands of the war, but they were also writing a constitution for their state, Massachusetts.

Bett was often ill-tempered. "I am beginning to understand what Josiah and Grippy meant about how these people make a difference between laws that have to do with people and those that have to do with property. The rights of the people will not be decided by all of the people, but only by those who own property."

I listened, but I didn't care about their laws. I was worried about Nance, who was not at all well. And about Josiah. We hadn't heard from him in a long time. We didn't know whether he was dead or alive. The only thing we heard was that the Africans in the war could not sign up for just three months; they had to sign up for the duration. Josiah had been gone now for more than a year and we had received only one letter.

"Aissa," Bett said, "I heard them talking about raising money for the families of soldiers in the war. Wouldn't that be nice?"

"You think the master will let you have your share?"

"I don't know, but they seem to be concerned more than other colonies. And they are angry, too. They're doing more and getting less credit. They don't like that General Washington. They wanted somebody named John Hancock, but their own representative there in Philadelphia, John Adams, chose Washington."

"I don't want to hear that. The only soldier I want to hear about is Josiah."

Bett rushed from the room, leaving me and Little Bett alone in the darkness. I knew I had hurt her feelings. She always refused to talk about things that might let me know that she had feelings like the rest of us.

The next time I was sent into the main street for oil, candles, and other items for the house, I saw men marching up and down with guns practicing for war. Some as young as fifteen. I heard they had to have their own guns. Some of them had big rifles, and others had what appeared to be guns for shooting birds. Little John told his father that he wanted to sign up, but the mistress would hear nothing of that. She would buy him a replacement first.

There was some excitement in the house one day when Little John walked in with a young man about his own age. The two were having lively talk and I could tell the friend was not a gentleman's son. The mistress was sitting in the room and when she heard the chatter, she stood. John was sort of taken back with surprise, but the other young man stood smiling, waiting, I thought, for John to say something.

"Don't stand there with your cap on like the ruffian you are. Remove your cap in my presence," the mistress said, coldly.

The young man, confused, stood with a look of disbelief on his face, then he jerked the cap from his head, leaving his hair untidy. Finally

John said, "Mother, this is Simon. He will be going to war soon. I want him to see my guns. Come with me, Simon." John spoke as if the outburst had not occurred.

"I must be on my way," Simon said, squaring his shoulders. "I feel I'd be intruding if I stayed. But thank you anyway. Maybe I'll see your guns in battle." He stuffed his cap back on his head and was about to leave the room.

"Wait," the mistress said. "I will give you sixty pounds if you will agree to take John's place in the service."

"Sixty pounds?"

"His father will add more, I am sure, if that is not enough."

"Enough for what?" the master said as he walked into the room.

"This young man is willing to take John's place in service."

"And who said John's place is for sale?" the master asked. "Is this your doing, John?"

"I brought him here to see my guns because he is off soon. It's not my idea."

"I'm sorry, sir," Simon said. "There's a mistake. I'm going in my own place." He hurried off.

"John," the master said, "you are excused."

After John left, the master said to the mistress, "Why did you assume John will not do his duty as a soldier when it is time?"

"Because I don't want him to," she cried.

"It's not left up to you, or to me. It is strictly his decision and I don't want you to interfere. Is that clear?"

I soon left the house for chores away from the mistress, for I knew she was angry at the master and my very presence could easily spark a violent storm.

Nance got no better, and when Sarah came in for sewing she helped Nance with the cooking. Sarah did the strenuous things like kneading bread and lifting heavy pans out of the oven. Her news was sad. More and more men were joining the service, including Agrippa.

That year, 1778, we had an early fall and the days were cold and damp. With few men to harvest the fields and orchards, the mistress and the girls had to help. The mistress did no picking; she took the pails back and forth to the cart that held the picked fruit. I was surprised to see that she was getting older and still she hadn't learned to control her temper.

Though Nance had been coughing and had

a fever, she had to come into the orchard to
help pick the fruit. I tried to work close to her
and put fruit in her pail so that the mistress
would not complain. I was off at the cart with
a pail of pickings and when I returned, Nance
had fallen, facedown, and could not get up.

"Come, boy," the mistress called to Brom.
"Take her to her quarters and hurry back to
work."

"I'll go with her to see that she's all right,"
Bett said.

"She'll be fine. We must get this fruit picked."

"Mother," Mary said, alarmed. "I'll go with
her."

"You will do no such thing. I am sure she'll
be all right."

It was late when we returned to our room.
Immediately we went to see about Nance. She
was unable to talk, but groaned as if in great
pain. Bett went for the master. When he saw
Nance he said, "Why have you waited so long
to tell me she was sick?"

"When she fell in the orchard, the mistress
said she'd be all right and that I must keep
working."

"When did this happen?"

"Just before midday meal."

He sighed deeply. "A doctor could have been called then. I'll have to wait until morning now."

We sat all night. Just before the cock crowed, Nance became quiet and I fell asleep. Day was dawning when Bett awoke me. "Nance is dead," she said.

"She can't be. She can't leave us now." I began to cry.

"Aissa, don't. Let her spirit depart in peace. For sure, Nance is now free. Let us rejoice in her freedom."

I could not rejoice. I could only feel angry that nothing had been done to make sure that nothing could be done.

Nance's funeral was held in the early evening on a warm autumn day so that other slaves could come after their work. The mistress gave Bett cotton to make a winding sheet and the master provided a coffin. The men brought wood to make torches to lighten the dark. A friend, Felix Cato, who was also a Methodist preacher, was asked to do the service.

We all met around the coffin that lay on a trestle in front of the building where we lived. Only Mary came from the house. She stood with us, a small figure, her fair hair falling to her shoulders, and listened silently as we all lifted our voices in a hymn. When the prayer was said, we knelt in the soft grass and sand. At first Mary seemed uncertain, then she sank to her knees.

Minister Felix closed his prayer with a blessing upon the master and mistress and upon the little mistress who had graced us with her presence.

I glanced at Mary. Her head was lowered, her face and neck scarlet, and tears were beginning to flow. In this act of facing God, did she accept us as equals? The full moon hung golden on the horizon as we walked to the small plot where slaves were buried, under the sound of those words that assured us that there was a resurrection and life, and those who died would live again. After prayer and song at the grave, Minister Felix said a few words, once more assuring us that Nance would live again. "Didn't God raise Lazarus from the dead?" he asked in his deep, spellbinding voice. "Then why not our sister, Nance?"

It was not until the body was lowered into the ground that we all sensed our loss and poured out our grief in cries and lamentations, Little Bett most piteously. My sister stood dry-eyed and Mary looked amazed and a little frightened at our outcry, but she stayed until we were all ready to walk back.

Mary walked alone ahead of us and went directly home. For a few minutes we stood about while Bett expressed our thanks to all for coming. The full moon was now a cold white light as we said good-bye to our friends and went to our room.

We quietly undressed and while we were saying our prayers, Bett broke down and cried. "Oh, if only there was someone I could turn to who'll be there."

I wanted to take her in my arms and assure her that she could turn to me. I was there for her, but I could not move, and the moment was lost forever.

21

After Nance's death, the mistress tried to make a cook out of Bett. Bett had never been a kitchen person. She was always lady's maid, housekeeper, errand-runner, plus assistant to the master. I was at my best alone, outside in the field. The master often came by and looked at my work. My rows were straight and always shaped so that the water settled to nourish the roots. I made ditches nearby to hold water that could be used when we had a dry spell. He noticed, but never said anything. Where I worked, the yield was better. I knew if I had owned land, I would have been a good farmer.

I was also a good cook. I had spent too many years in the kitchen not to have learned from

146

Nance. But did the mistress ask if I could cook? She did not. And I didn't tell her. The less she expected of me, the less I had to do. She expected me to be stupid and so I fulfilled her expectations.

With Bett in the kitchen, we suffered. The bread was heavy, the gravy lumpy, the meat over- or underdone. There was never a leaving-the-table feeling full and satisfied. Finally, the mistress hired Sarah.

Nance had been a good basic cook; Sarah was a fancy one. She had worked in many different homes: the Kellogs', Callenders', Ingersolls', and Deweys'. Therefore, she brought to the Ashleys' a range of new ideas that Sarah called her own. I learned much from her and more about her.

At first, I found it hard to work with her. She had her own way of doing things. She seldom used the wooden sour tub for making bread, and when she did, she used honey and salted it strong. "You must wash all the silver before you do the dishes," she always reminded me. "And wash the glassware before the china." What difference did it make? All things had to be washed. I learned that if I did it Sarah's way, it was easier and the dishes looked cleaner.

Sarah could read and write. Sometimes she made things from a book that she hid under her skirt so that the mistress would not take it away from her. Her pastries were crumbly good, her pheasant was never dry, and the way she used wines made all of the mistress's guests wonder what she did to make things taste so good. Sarah never showed her book.

One day I saw her reading and said to her, "Sarah, do you think I could learn to read?"

"You learned to talk, didn't you? I remember when you came you couldn't speak English at all. You and your sister spoke Dutch. You learned to speak English, I would say too fast." She laughed.

"What's that got to do with reading?"

"Everything. The words we say are made out of letters." She wrote an X, an A, and a T. "People let the X stand for their names when they can't write. You know what a bird is. B-I-R-D stands for that creature that sings. So you see, writing is nothing but things standing for things. We call them words. You read words, and anybody who talks as much as you, girl, can read."

I began to pay attention. But the mistress didn't let up for one minute. There was always something that I had not done, or had not done right. But when she was not around, Sarah and I found time for me to learn to read. What joy!

My sister was happy that I was happy, but she did not get along with Sarah as well as she had with Nance. Nance was motherly, Sarah youthfully fresh. Sarah knew a lot, but I soon learned that she did not have the wisdom my sister had. And my sister knew that. I also learned a lot about my sister, looking at her alongside Sarah. She treated Sarah the way she treated most people, friendly but always held at a distance. Bett never made small talk, and she could talk all day and never say enough about herself to give you a clue to who she really was.

Sarah admired her, but there was some competition between the slave and the hired woman. The very first day, Sarah said, "Miss Bett, can you come and show me how to set up for the guest?" Bett in her most friendly manner said, "I am neither miss nor mistress in this house. About things like that you must speak to Mistress Anna." She smiled and walked quickly from the room.

Sarah soon learned that Bett would not oversee her work, nor was Bett interested in what

was going on in the kitchen. She had her chores
on and off the place that kept her busy, and
besides, even though she didn't show it, I knew
she was deeply worried about Josiah. A whole
year had gone by since we had last heard from
him.

Fall turned to cold, rainy, icy winter. Long after
our prayers for Josiah were over, I struggled by
candlelight, bundled in my clothes and old blan-
kets, to read the worn primer and speller that
Sarah had given me. Bit by bit I learned the
miracle of reading and writing.

What joy I found reading to Little Bett. My
sister had almost no time with us, but sometimes when snow was falling and the wind was
whistling in the trees, she, too, was delighted
with the prayers and Bible stories.

Sarah brought word that wounded soldiers
were returning from the slave battalion. Bett
and I began to hope that maybe Josiah would
be among them, or that we would have word
from him. We waited.

One evening we all were together in the
room that had once belonged to Nance, talking,
remembering Josiah and the men we had known
who had been gone so long. "Listen," Brom

said. Everyone hushed, and a soft knock sounded. We remained quiet, for we expected no one at that time of night. Brom cautiously opened the door, and Sarah and a thin man with haunting eyes came into the room. His clothes were in tatters, his shoes worn, and he had a terrible cough.

Sarah introduced him as Quam Tanner, and Bett gave him her name and asked him to sit. He smiled and relaxed a little when he sat down. "Miss Freeman," he said, "I have searched for you a long time. Your husband asked me to find you and say that he is well and to give you a letter."

"Oh, praises be," Bett shouted.

"Hallelujah!" we all cried in response.

"Where did you see him?" I asked.

"We were together in New York near West Point. The going was rough, but not as rough as in other places. His troop was scheduled to join Colonel Christopher Green."

"How bad is it?" Brom asked.

"Depends on who's telling. Bad enough, but we had some good times. I hear you know Grippy. Wherever Grippy is, there is going to be some fun. Grippy had gotten in with General Paterson. There was this General Kosciusko who really liked Grippy, so General Paterson let Kosciusko have Grippy as his servant. Grippy took care of the general's clothes, which were expensive and very pompous. There was even a three-cornered hat covered with ostrich plumes."

"You sure he was a general?" Brom asked, and we all laughed.

"Where was he from?" I asked.

"From Poland." Quam went on. "Now one night the general left the Point saying he was going 'cross the river and wouldn't be back for two or three days. Grippy got busy and cooked a dinner and invited us all over, Josiah included. When we arrived, Grippy was all dressed up in the general's expensive uniform, hat and all. We were having a good time when all of a sudden the general came into the room. Man, we were jumping out windows, getting out of there. Grippy was so embarrassed."

"And I bet that general was some angry," Brom said.

"No, he wasn't. He paraded his servant around and introduced him as an African prince who was a great warrior. I think Grippy would rather have had a whipping."

I could see the dignified Agrippa Hull being

caught in such an outfit. I joined the others in laughter.

Bett sat as if she were not aware that we were in the room. It didn't cross her mind that we were as anxious as she to know what Josiah had to say in his letter. She folded it in her skirt and sat as if it didn't exist. Sarah and the guest soon said good night.

When we reached our room, Bett hurriedly removed the letter and thrust it at me. "Read it!"

I trembled. What if I could not read a letter? I had only read from books. And Sarah had gone. Would my sister dare call Little John?

"Read it!" she said with such command in her voice that I knew I would. And I did:

My dear Wife, Sister, and Daughter:
It has been so long that I fear you don't remember me. I am well, considering this bloody business. I am blessed that my clothes are still holding up. My shoes are worn, but still protect my feet. But like all the other men, I am without ample food. There is no quartermaster so we have no supplies. And when we buy anything out of our little stipend, we are forced to pay 100 times more than it is worth. People are getting rich while the army that

is fighting for them is starving. I want you to go and ask for the stipend they have promised to all families of fighting men. I am sure your master will know about this. Let us pray that he will let you have it. Our battalion has no hope of getting out of this until it is over. There is no such thing as three months for us. We are fighting and fighting hard. But it will all be worthwhile if I know in the end you and all of our people will be free. Let us pray that Divine Power will bring us together again so that we can love each other in peace.
Your husband, father, and brother,
Josiah

Next morning, the mistress was already up and dressed in a heavy cloak, walking up and down between the kitchen and dining room. Her eyes were swollen with tears. "Hurry and light the kitchen fire," she shouted at Little Bett. "Nothing is going right around here."

There were muddy footprints leading up the stairs to the bedrooms, so I knew that guests had come in the night. "Lizzie, light the fire in my and the master's rooms, but do not enter the others. I am tired of all this coming and going." She began to cry.

"What is it, Meesteres Annetje?" It pleased

the mistress when Bett spoke to her in the mistress's language.

"Oh, Bett, John has decided that he is going away to this bloody war. I've talked to him until I'm blue in the face, but neither he nor his father will give in. He's determined to go."

"He's a man, and men think they are made to fight. Oh, how I wish people could settle their problems without all this killing."

"It is unholy," the mistress cried.

Before we had finished lighting fires or had the water boiling, Major Fellows was knocking on the door. "Is John ready? We must be on our way."

"He is not going!" the mistress screamed.

But Little John was dressed in his uniform and had seen to it that Brom had saddled his big bay horse. He carried a backpack made of canvas and his gun with powder horn and many pellets. Tired of her ranting, he was off before the mistress had time to complain to him directly.

I thought of Josiah and it was a sad moment for us all. The news brought by the men who had come in the night was not good. One was a heavy man with dark eyes and long dark hair.

When he came down for breakfast, his presence filled the room and I knew that he was someone special.

"Who's that man?" I asked my sister.

"That's Tapping Reeve, the lawyer from Connecticut I told you about."

Around the table that morning there was much talk about the soldiers being angry about no supplies, and no pay, and their losing war. Their discontent was likely to lead to mutiny.

"The problem," one of the guests stated, "is the poor quality of our officers. Many of them are deserting along with thousands of recruits. And our forces are under foreigners who are bounty seekers."

One of the men asked the question, "Is it true that bounty seekers are getting rich?"

I listened, hoping one of them would say what bounty was. He went on, "I hear men are taking cash money for signing up in one county, serving for a few days, deserting, and going into another county for cash."

Lawyer Reeve, who was outspoken, answered. "Yes, they're bounty seekers. But the real problem is that taxes are too high and it's the poor who are bearing the burden of this war."

I was amazed. He spoke in a voice that was just a whisper, but his words were spoken in such a way that one could not mistake his soft voice for a weakness. He continued. "You here in Massachusetts are sharing the burden more equally, but overall others are not."

"We organized for paying our share early in the war," the master said.

"Too many who refuse to fight are getting rich," Lawyer Reeve said. "And even here there are some who are growing rich while suffering none of the hardships and danger. I wouldn't be surprised if the army turned arms against the rich and set up a just government."

There was a threatening silence. Then he said, "Life will not go on as before, whether we win or lose this war. The poor are angry as they struggle, and I believe the silent millions will one day speak the living words of history."

I looked at Bett. She stood still, listening as if entranced. I thought, This is what she hears all the time, those high-sounding words from guests, but never the simple statement: Slaves must be free.

A few days later, Bett spoke to the master about the stipend due her because Josiah was a soldier.

"You're not legally married, Bett. You're a slave," he said.

Bett shifted her weight and sighed. "But my husband is a free man," she told him quietly.

"There are many women legally married whose husbands are fighting, who get no pay. There is no money. Some soldiers have not been paid since 1777. You are well taken care of. Many are begging bread." He walked away, closing the subject.

I pretended I hadn't heard, but I began to notice. Some of the women who came to wash were in tatters. Their children's faces were drawn and thin, their arms and legs like sticks. These women were getting no help. And as the winter closed in, some came to the mistress's door begging bread. Sarah took the liberty to share without the mistress's permission.

22

The winter of 1778 was the coldest I had ever known. Ice formed on everything. On trees it glistened and sparkled red, blue, and green lights that were almost blinding. The ground froze hard and the rutted roads were sharp enough to cut the feet. It was in the midst of this cold spell that we received another letter from Josiah. The writing was difficult to read, as if it had been painfully written:

Bett, my dear:

I hope when you get this letter things will be much better for me. We have joined the main troops under General Washington in Valley Forge. We are in dire straits for food and clothing. I made the mistake to take off my shoes to try to dry my feet and someone stole them. I stripped my blanket to wrap my feet, but they are now frozen, turning black. Without my blanket, I am never warm. We get no supplies and many men are naked, many covered with vermin and riddled with diseases. People who see us call us the ragged, lousy, naked regiment. And our French allies make jokes at the expense of our nudity. More than three thousand of us are unfit for duty. We are fighting still, even though many are dying for lack of medicine and care. Worst of all, we are not paid. I hope you were able to get our share there. Whatever money you get, I beg you to use it for yours and Ayisha's freedom. Say to Ayisha that my love for her and my determination for her freedom keep me going.

I worry about her and Aissa. But not about you. I feel you are capable of taking care of things. Needless to say I love you and long for the day when we will be together again. Pray for peace and for us who feel as though we are the forgotten wretched.

Much love.
Josiah

That letter pushed us into silence. I could not say what I was feeling for fear of breaking into sobs. I had a strong sense that we would never see Josiah again. I knew that Bett felt the same. She held her child more closely than ever, as if feeling her loss. It wasn't long before what we secretly dreaded fell upon us.

One Sunday we were walking back from my sister's place early in the evening. Feathery clouds were pink from the glow of the setting sun. We were quiet as we came to the edge of the master's land. Mary was waiting for us. She was always serious, but today there was a sadness in her face. "Bett, Father would like to see all of you in his office right away," she said.

Was he angry? I wondered. What had we done to displease him? I wanted to ask Mary, but I didn't want her to know the guilt that always arose in me whenever the master summoned, even though I had done nothing wrong.

When we arrived at the house, the master and mistress were in the waiting room. They rose immediately and asked us to come with them up the stairs. Suddenly I knew something was terribly wrong. My heart pounded in my stomach, making me weak. The master took a piece of paper from his desk and handed it to Bett. "Bett, uh . . . it's Josiah. . . . Word has come. He is dead." He did not look at my sister.

Little Bett let out a cry that pierced the heart more than the ear. One cry, then silence. I felt faint, but held on for my sister, who I could see was crumbling inside. The mistress kept her head lowered and I sensed a feeling of sympathy from her that I had never felt before.

The paper he gave my sister listed Josiah's name, circled, as one from the areas of Sheffield and Stockbridge who had been listed as dead. That was all.

All night Bett and I cried, but after that sharp initial outcry, Little Bett remained stony silent. Bett wailed, sorely grieved that her husband, like our father and mother, had died among strangers and was buried in a strange land. But even worse, Josiah had not been among his people to prepare his body and help make that journey to the proper place. Oh, how I longed to go and search for his body and bring it here, where he had known some happiness in spite of all the pain and suffering that was the routine of our lives. Like my freedom — it wasn't to be.

It seemed the war would never end, and that the visitors would never stop coming. With John still away, the mistress was in no mood for parties and entertainment. However, she and the girls did join women in the town to make the shot pouches, fold garments, roll bandages, and pack water bottles. The master was away often, and the slaves and other workers kept the place going.

There was much excitement when the master was at home. Bett was busy going back and forth upstairs seeing to it that the men who were working on the Massachusetts constitution were served rum, tea, and wine. The meetings were long, with much talk. Sometimes we heard them in the kitchen.

"What is all the fuss?" Sarah asked when Bett came for more rum, which was popular since tea was still scarce.

"They are arguing over a list of rights and freedoms they think are good for the people of this state — what they call a 'bill of rights.' They say the first constitution for Massachusetts was defeated by the voters because it didn't have that bill. And some of them up there want a bill of rights, but they want more to make sure that property owners will not lose any power to those without property."

How my sister could be interested in all of that was a mystery to me. All I wanted to know was whether the war was over and who had won. Even though Josiah had given his life for the

Colonials, and even though Governor Gage had not signed that bill, I was still torn between the British and the Colonials. It didn't matter to me who won; all I wanted was the end of slavery. But Bett felt there was something in the constitution for people who had little and for slaves who had nothing. She was definitely on the side of the Colonials.

"I hear a lot about it, but they don't tell us much. There is little in the few newspapers," Sarah said.

"The bill of rights states that all men are born equally free, that each man has certain rights, and that all are bound to obey only those laws to which they have given their consent."

"Why're you so excited? You're not a man. They're not talking about us, Bett," I said.

"That doesn't mean just men, it means *people*, men and women," Bett replied.

"Most of the men upstairs will say that, but they are not about to make it a part of their lives. They are the rulers and they will never give up their property. Of course the poor can be equal when fighting in the army," Sarah said. She spoke as if she knew them well.

"They're asking up there if the poor can do anything but fight in the army," Bett said. "Can they make decisions about property when they have none? Their answer is no. It's only them, the educated and property owners, who have the wisdom," Bett said.

"They're the same people in the courts who would not give us our freedom, so how will it be different this time?" I asked.

"This time it's not left up to the court and the king. The people will vote and every free man twenty-one years old and older will be voting on that constitution. They have to talk about it in every town. That's why they are so busy upstairs. They want to have their way in the town meetings and get all they can for themselves. But we'll see how the people vote."

"Why do they have to go through all that for just some bill of rights?" Sarah asked.

"There are lots of other things that are important to them: What church will be the main one, who will pay taxes, things like that."

"Won't matter. The poor will be poor, and we'll still be slaves." I was not that interested.

"Lizzie, you have *no* faith. I have to believe that if it is said, it can be done. If all of us are created equal, then we all have the same rights to life. I have to believe that. Otherwise I couldn't go on living, knowing that Josiah died

for nothing." She went hurriedly upstairs. She
must not keep them waiting.

That night she came home very excited.
"That lawyer, Tapping Reeve, was there, and
when he was leaving he said to me that he was
sorry that I had lost my husband in the war.

"I was so surprised, I hardly spoke above a
whisper when I thanked him. But I calmed myself and asked if he knew whether I could get
Josiah's pay or a wife's stipend.

"He seemed surprised that I had not been
given anything. He said he would look into it
for me and see what he could get. You see, I
have faith that there are good people everywhere, you just have to know how to be open
to receive that goodness."

"He hasn't done anything for you yet."

"He promised. For me, that is enough to hold
on to my faith."

The meetings upstairs went on. Tapping Reeve
kept his promise and Bett received the twenty
pounds offered to families in the state of Massachusetts and forty shillings from the Continental Army, two months of Josiah's pay. She
was so happy, and wasted no time before going
to the master to ask to purchase Little Bett. He

laughed. Did she not know how little money that was? Twenty pounds would not purchase any slave. He could raise five times that much for a healthy slave child. His answer was a firm *no*.

Finally after many town meetings, in 1780, the Massachusetts Constitution was finished and voted for. Bett told me that anybody voting for state officials had to own *twice* as much property as they had had to own before the constitution was written; and that to vote they had to pay something called a poll tax, which could be raised at any time.

I said to her, "But you said the people would decide that, not the court. How could the people vote to double the amount needed to vote? And why would they want to pay to vote? Did they really vote for that?"

"Yes, and two-thirds had to agree to all of it." My sister refused to be upset. "They got the bill of rights."

"They deserved something." My tone did not tell her, in the least, the way I felt, and we closed that conversation without her reminding me of my impatience and lack of faith.

On November 25, one month before our

days off at Christmas, a terrible thing happened.
We were finishing up in the orchards and with
other odds and ends when I heard an argument
between Zach and the master. Suddenly the
master took his rifle from his saddle and handed
it to his white foreman. While the foreman held
the gun, the master beat Zach in the face and
across the head, and when Zach fell, he kicked
him. We watched. I felt frightened and help-
lessly angry.

Then the master called the constable, who
took Zach away and put him in prison. We
didn't know what to do or where to go to see
him. So each night we added Zach to our prayers along with all the others we knew wearing
the yoke.

23

Bett went about her duties in the house as if she had not been denied the right to own her child. And as if her husband had not given his life for a mere twenty pounds, forty shillings. When the master asked, she gave. When the mistress commanded, she responded as though she was there only to serve. Sometimes I wanted to scream at her, You are more than just a slave! My anger burned like white heat while she remained cool. Was she biding her time? Did she know something that I didn't know?

At times I could see the disrespect Sarah felt for my sister, thinking that Bett accepted slavery willingly. After Bett had sought to buy Little Bett's freedom, the mistress had made life as miserable as possible for my sister. One day we were doing general cleaning. Bett was dusting windowsills.

"Bett," the mistress asked, "when did you oil this dining table?"

"Just yesterday, Mistress."

"Then do it again."

"Yes, Mistress." Bett went on dusting.

"Did you hear me, Bett? Do it again."

Before Bett had finished the table, the mistress called from upstairs. "Bett, these bed-clothes need airing badly."

"Yes, Mistress. As soon as I finish the table."

"Finish the table later. Do this bedding now!"

Bett started up the stairs. Sarah said, "Slow down. She pays me, and she'd better not do that to me. Finish that table."

Bett ignored Sarah and went up the stairs. Sarah sighed and said to me, "Too bad your sister doesn't have your nerve. I bet if you were not a girl, you would've run away by now."

I was ashamed but, even though I sometimes felt that Bett had too much patience in that house, I defended her. "My sister has the strength and the wisdom that I would do well to have. My impatience is a weakness." Sarah never again hinted that my sister bowed to the master and mistress.

The war went on without either side being able to win a decisive victory. The house was in turmoil. The mistress daily confronted the master about getting John out of the service and with other matters that were trivial to say the least. I will never forget one day in March. The wind whipped up clouds that threatened a storm. I knew those clouds could bring hail as big as small donkers. But we had to remain in the field. Suddenly Zach was before us, as if he had been blown in by the wind. How happy we were to see him. His wounds were healed, but there were scars to remind us of that awful day.

In April, Bett came to our room. "Lord, trouble never seems to end. Listen to this: Zach Mullen has gone to the courts and accused the master of abuse and imprisonment. He is asking for the sum of nine pounds and nineteen shillings. They're going to court when it meets in August."

"What? Bett, why can't we go? We're slaves. The mistress has beat me and she's always saying mean, nasty things."

"The master beat Zach under the gun. But the court will decide." While Zach waited, he still worked and the master kept his distance.

One evening, not long after Zach returned, we were in our room. I was reading to my niece and sister when someone knocked on our door. I rushed to open it. There in his uniform, with his sword by his side, stood John. He was so pale, and he looked years older. He smiled and asked, "May I come in?"

Bett jumped up, pulled him into the room, and put her arms around him. As she hugged him, tears flowed down his cheeks. "I'm so glad to be home," he said, and looked embarrassed.

Bett told him that she had lost her husband, and they cried some more.

"Are you home for good?" Bett asked.

"Unfortunately. I can no longer be the best soldier, because of a head wound."

I thought of the little boy who used to act like Bett was his mother, and watched the young man now made old by war and I felt his pain.

One lovely morning in May, not long after Little John returned, we were together in the kitchen. Brom had come to saddle John's favorite horse for John to go for a ride. After her son had left, the mistress, tearful, went to her room as she always did after watching him do anything. The girls went to help roll bandages and make the canvas bags for soldiers still at war.

All seemed well, and we were ready to have breakfast before going to work. Sarah had prepared a fine meal, including fresh scones. Little Bett, Bett, Brom, Sarah, and I began eating in a happy mood.

"Brom," Sarah said, "I saw you far from here with a pretty girl."

"You didn't see me with a girl," Brom said. "Wasn't me."

"Brom," Bett said, "tell the truth and shame the devil."

"Now, Bett, you know I love to brag. If I had a pretty woman, I certainly would tell."

During pleasant moments when you forget you're a slave, the rude jerk back to reality is always a blow to the spirit. The mistress, hearing our laughter, burst in on us and said, "No one has declared time off for you. Bett, I would think you had better sense than to let this happen. Up from here, all of you, and get to work."

Everyone rose to go, but I couldn't bring my-

self to move. Why would my mind refuse to
send the signal to my feet? Move! All the others
froze, knowing that I was putting myself in danger. The mistress was not to be disobeyed and
never confronted. Still I could not move. It was
as though time and motion slowed. The mistress
shivered with anger; then she grabbed the
shovel that had been left in the coals. The metal
gleamed red and flashed as she seemed to float
toward me, the shovel raised at my head.

Bett screamed and ran between me and the
red-hot shovel. It landed on her arm just above
the elbow, and the stench of burning flesh filled
the room. For a moment I heard and saw nothing. Then the bedlam. Brom grabbed the shovel
and Bett screamed, "No!"

Calmly, he placed the shovel on the hearth
and quickly left the room. "Oh, Bett," the mistress cried. She moved toward my sister.

"Please, don't." Bett stepped away. "Come,
Little Bett. Come, Aissa." That was the first
time she had ever called my name in front of
the mistress. "Come, we're going home."

"You can't leave here. You belong in this
house."

"I belong in *my* house! And if you call the

constable, I will charge you for cruel treatment of your slave."

"Are you threatening me?"

"No threat, mistress. I merely state the truth. I'm leaving and I'll never come back."

Then I realized what I had done. I had placed my sister and brother in danger. My sister's arm, seared, was white to the bone. What if my brother had hit the mistress? He would have been hanged.

I saw my sister in a different light as I packed our things to go to her house. The blow to Bett's arm was severe. I somehow felt that it was as much to her pride as to her arm. I was so ashamed and hurt. But how grateful I was to her for not letting Brom defend us. How sad for him that he, as a slave, could not protect his sisters.

When we were well down the road, Brom came through the forest and joined us. He took our bundles so that I could support Bett who was in shock. Bett collapsed in pain as soon as we reached her place. She tried hard to disguise it, but I knew she was suffering. What would happen to us? The master was probably setting things in motion to make us return.

The deep wound that had been seared white was now scarlet like the flame that had heated the shovel. And what should have been blood was a clear liquid oozing around it. In spite of the pain, Bett was able to tell me what herbs to mix that would help prevent infection. That night I was so busy trying to relieve Bett's pain that I had no time to worry about the master.

Next morning I was the first to hear the sound of a horse-drawn cart. "Bett, he's coming. Let's hide."

"I don't know who it is, but no matter, I will not hide." She got up and went to the door. It was the master, and before he had a chance to get down from the cart, Bett met him. "I will not go back to a place where our lives are in danger," she said even before he spoke.

"I have never raised a hand to you. You have been treated with respect and with kindness in my house."

"You've not beaten me, but I've done nothing to deserve a beating. I've worked hard and long for you and your wife's family. For that I've not earned one pence. The work I did for others, you were paid for that. That's not respect nor kindness. I've suffered the abuse your wife heaped upon my sister and finally upon me." She showed him her arm.

He winced, his face reddened, and he spoke harshly. "You will return with me now or I will call the constable and have you brought back."

"I think the constable would agree with me that I've been abused, and you have no right to abuse a slave. I'll stay right here until the constable comes."

I listened, so afraid. What if they put us in jail? I felt that my life with my sister was over. The mistress would probably insist that I be sold off to Barbados or down south. Not long after the master left, the constable came and arrested us all and took us to the master's.

Sarah greeted us and insisted that Bett sit down. "The mistress is getting dressed," she whispered. "She knows you all were coming so she'll be down soon."

I sat in a corner, hoping the mistress would ignore my presence. The mistress rushed to Bett. "Oh, Bett. How are you? Let me see that arm."

"My arm is painful," Bett said matter-of-factly. "It's not good to uncover it." She refused to show the wound.

"Bett," the mistress cried. "Bett, you know I'd do nothing to harm you. I lost my temper." She looked around the room and when she saw me, she went stiff and no words would come. I fled the room.

I joined others at work in the fields, but Bett could do no work with that arm. My sister was quiet, and when I tried to talk to her, she refused to talk. We were busy trying to keep her arm from getting worse. Luckily Bett knew how to keep the wound clean and loosely wrapped to let it air. The herbs and salves were healing, but the scar tissue had to be removed daily to keep the wound from pulling the arm out of shape with the scarring. It was very painful. At night I heard her praying, but mostly for our release.

24

Two weeks later, we asked permission to go with Brom to Bett's farm to pick up our belongings. The master consented. On the way, Brom was quiet.

"What is it, Brom?" I asked.

"I'm ashamed that I could not protect you and Bett."

"Don't be ashamed, Brom," Bett said. "To have hit her would have meant your death. I could not bear losing you, too," Bett said.

"But what am I worth if I can't protect my sisters? Just breathing is not a life. Bett, I'm a man."

"Surely you are, Brom." Then we were silent. As if speaking to herself, Bett said, "I meant what I said. I'm not going back!" She looked at

Brom. "I have the money from Josiah; he
wanted me to use it to buy freedom. That constitution that says we are all born free and equal
means you and me. We're going to see a lawyer."

"You're a woman and can't stand in the
courts," Brom said.

"Brom, you can," I said.

"We'll do it together," Bett promised.

So instead of going for our things, we set out
to find the only lawyer near that Bett knew.
There was no certainty that he would even listen, but there wasn't much time, and I sensed
that Bett had to act now for fear of losing control of the situation. She must not wait.

We walked a great distance to get to the Sedgwick place. It was late when we arrived. The
house was nothing like the master's but it was
well built for comfort.

Before Brom knocked on the door, Bett
looked at me and said, "Let me do all the talking
unless I ask you to say something." A young
girl answered the door, with a look of surprise
to see Brom and the rest of us on the steps.
She asked us in and went immediately for her
father. I noticed a wan woman on a small cot;
she had dark circles under her large, pale eyes.

Master Sedgwick invited us into a small room crowded with a desk and books in shelves on the wall. We stood while Bett told him that she wanted to obtain his help to win her freedom.

"I am not sure I can help you. There is no specific law on which I can base your case."

"What about the constitution that states we are all born free and equal?"

He looked surprised. "What do you know about the constitution?" he asked.

"I keep quiet and listen. I heard what was said in Master Ashley's house. On what I heard, I believe we can be freed."

"Bett, you know that your master is my friend. He is good to his servants, and both he and your mistress think the world of you. They always brag about what a good servant you are and how they could not do without your help."

Bett smiled and I thought, Surely Bett knows we are not servants; we are slaves, and the master and mistress are not good to us.

The lawyer went on, "Besides, there being no specific law, I'm afraid I would not want to take a case against a fine, outstanding citizen who is also a judge."

"Maybe there is no law. But the people wanted a law to say that slavery is wrong. Twice they asked for such a law, and the king and his governors said no," Bett said.

As she was speaking, the lawyer, Tapping Reeve, was led into the room. "Why, Tapping, how good to see you. Bear with me," Lawyer Sedgwick said. "These people will be leaving in a minute."

"I'm in your area on a case and wanted to say hello. Don't let me interrupt what must be business." He turned to Bett. "I run into you everywhere in this town."

"She is quite a person, a good servant to our friend Judge Ashley."

"Slave, not servant," I said.

Bett gave me a withering look and said, "Mr. Reeve, my sister is for saying aloud what she thinks. Please don't mind her."

"So am I, and there *is* a difference between servant and slave," Reeve said.

"Yes," Sedgwick said, "and, Tapping, knowing you, it may be of interest that Bett is here seeking freedom under our state's constitution. I told her that there is nothing specific in that document that grants a slave's right to freedom."

"Hmm, that is most interesting," Reeve answered.

"It is interesting, but I hesitate because she has no complaints of any abuse. Her master is a good, kind man who does justice by his servants."

Why does he keep saying "servants"? I wondered. We are slaves! I wanted to remind him again. He went on. "There is absolutely no proof that there has been abuse."

I waited for Bett to show them that ugly wound. Bett sat, her chest rising and falling; she was like a dam filled to overflowing. Show them! I wanted to shout to her. Then Bett said, "Words describing a *good* and *kind* master do not go together when talking about slavery." Her voice broke as she said, "With or without wounds, we deserve to be free."

"Please," I said, looking at Bett crying, "my sister is not crying for your pity. She wants only justice, which she feels can come in that bill of rights."

"Maybe we can make hers *the* test case to see if your constitution with its bill of rights is more than words — a working law capable of ending slavery," Reeve said.

"We might be able to do something by appealing to the sentiments of the people as Bett has suggested, and this time end this slave business under the constitution," Master Sedgwick said.

"I'll be happy to join you in defense of her. But can a woman stand in your courts?" Reeve asked.

Bett spoke quickly. "My brother, Brom, here is willing to stand, sir, and the money you were kind enough to help me get will pay the fees."

"Oh, don't worry about money," Sedgwick said. "If we win we'll insist that Colonel Ashley pay the fees and pay you something, too. This case can be a groundbreaker."

As we were leaving, the woman on the cot beckoned to Bett, and Bett urged us to go on as she went to speak to her. We walked the miles back and Brom and I said little. "Servants," he said, and nothing more, and I knew what he meant.

We were anxious to get back, but Bett took her time coming. What if the master came looking for us and found her at the Sedgwicks'? When Bett finally came, she reported, "That woman was Master Sedgwick's wife. She is in bad shape in both body and mind. Her baby is less than a year old and she's expecting another. I think I'll go and help her."

"How can you think of helping somebody

when you don't know what the master is up to?
How do you know we won't be going to jail or
be sold off somewhere?"

"He wouldn't dare. He's too well known and
wouldn't want people to know that his wife had
done such a thing. Besides, he is a judge himself, and has to respect the law."

"What law? They keep telling you we are
under no law," I said heatedly, for knowing Bett
I was afraid she might take this too lightly.

"They said they would take the case, so I am
not going to worry. I must heal my arm." That
was that. She refused to talk anymore about
what we were going to do.

When we arrived at the master's, Sarah was
waiting for us in our quarters. "The mistress is
very angry that you were allowed to go away.
'How do you know what they're up to?' she
screamed to the master. She was so afraid you
were not coming back. Don't be surprised if
she tightens the noose."

For days we were there as prisoners, working
around the place with our hearts not in the work
and our minds on nothing but being free. This
went on day after day, with the master and Little
John now keeping guard over us. Bett, because
of the wound, did little work.

Two weeks later, the sheriff came with a court order to remove Bett and Brom. The order stated that the two were being held against their will and could not be so detained unless they were taken by the court for a crime such as murder. The master had to state why he was holding them.

The master flatly refused to let them go. He stated his reason: Bett and Brom were his servants for life and he claimed a right to their servitude.

After the sheriff had come three times with an order to free them, and the master refused each time, on May 28, 1781, the stage was set for the matter to come to trial. The court ordered release, but only if Bett and Brom could post bond to guarantee that their case would continue.

My sister was happy that she had enough for the bond, but worried about paying the lawyers. The bond was paid. Bett and Brom were freed, and the sheriff issued a summons to the Ashleys to appear at the next regular session of the Court of Common Pleas on August 21. Little Bett, taking on the status of her mother, was allowed to go.

"What about me?" I asked the master when my sister and brother were released.

"The mistress will decide."

My heart felt swollen in my chest as it beat rapidly, and I felt weak. How could he put my fate in the hands of the mistress? He knew how she became like a whirlwind in a closet when I was around. This would be worse than Barbados. I did something that I had thought I would never do. "Please, master, let me live with my sister. You know that the mistress never wanted me. And I don't believe she is happy with me here. Please, let me go."

"Go. I will talk to the mistress, and if she wants you back, you will come. In the meantime you must understand that you owe me, and I expect you to pay, for the years of service you still have ahead."

I thought I would faint, but I held on. "Thank you, and I do understand."

25

We stayed at the house. Bett went about her duties with her arm loosely bandaged to keep air flowing to the wound. Whenever someone asked what was wrong with it, she replied, "Ask the mistress Ashley." She spent much of her time at the Sedgwicks', trying to get the children's mother well enough to perform the duties left to her when her husband was away, which was most of the time.

Brom and I worked our small plot and cleared more land around us that seemed to belong to no one, since much of the Indian land had been added to Sheffield and Great Barrington. I used my farming skills, making our plot look like the master's. We planted wheat, corn, squash, and potatoes, and cultivated the wild grapes and berries and apple trees on the place. We had only three maple trees, but if we were there the next spring we planned to bleed them and make syrup and sugar.

Little Bett blossomed, and I became her mother while Bett went daily to the Sedgwicks' and to other jobs. We were all grateful for work in the day. Our nights were spent wondering what was going to happen. I talked to Little Bett about freedom, and about that whispering man who was going to use the law to set us free.

We waited. Then one day Sarah came by. "The mistress is drowning in her sorrow. She can't pull herself together. She's now even claiming that Bett is the best cook in the world, not to mention housekeeper, nurse, and rippler of flax. When people ask what happened, she blames it all on you, Aissa, and your devilish ways."

"I hope she never asks me to come back," I said.

"They have been served notice that Bett and Brom are suing for their freedom. I think they are afraid to react, for the law is not clear. So they're waiting until their day in court. The master's hired David Noble from around here and

John Canfield of Connecticut, two fine lawyers. I think, however, he was stunned when his good friend, Theodore Sedgwick, took Bett's case and was joined by, of all people, Tapping Reeve, *the* best lawyer anywhere. Master Ashley has even resigned his judgeship."

"What is the mistress saying about all of this? She was proud to be a judge's wife," I said.

"The mistress is as mad as a wet hen. She dislikes the Sedgwicks. Claims he's haughty though his father was nothing but a humble shopkeeper. His brother had to sacrifice to send him to Yale. She says his wife is insane and can do nothing but have babies. In a special place in the house she even lets him keep a picture of his first wife, who died of chicken pox. Can you believe that? Ask Bett if that's true."

"My sister never talks about her patients. His wife is her patient now. If we learn the truth, it won't be from Bett."

In June of 1781, Bett came home with news that a slave, Quok Walker, had brought suit against his master, Nathaniel Jennison, for assault, and had won. Before Bett could finish telling us, Sarah, to our surprise, came to see us, bringing a cake, some homemade rum, and apple cider. "Celebration time," she said. She had heard the news at the Ashleys'. We had a great time and felt sure that Bett and Brom would win, and we all would be free.

Ayisha was now nine years old and a good worker. She had her father's smile, his good singing voice, and her mother's quiet poise; but there were moments, when she was crossed, she showed some of the fire that burned in me. I loved this child more than myself, and we worked well together.

Finally, in late August, word came that the court would, indeed, meet in Great Barrington on the twenty-first. Early on that morning, Brom, Bett, Little Bett, and I started the six-mile journey to Great Barrington. We dressed in our nicest calico, for the day was warm with the promise of heat ahead. Not knowing what to expect, we walked at a steady pace in silence. My mind was filled with doubts and fear. What if the court found no reason to free us and sent us back to the master? I tried to focus on the surroundings and the quiet of the forest, but I could not let go of the fear.

When we arrived at the court, Tapping Reeve greeted us. "Bett, it shouldn't be too long before we will be heard. The judge will hear arguments from the Ashleys' lawyer and from our side. You and Brom will sit up front with me. We will find a place in the back of the courtroom for your sister and your little girl. We are hoping that there will be enough people to serve on the jury and we will have no problem in the selection."

"Why would there be a problem?" Bett asked, alarmed.

"The Ashleys are prominent, well known. Some men might be reluctant to serve on a case that involves them. There are some who might want jobs, others who might be involved in trade with them. But don't you worry. I'm sure we'll work things out all right."

Little Bett and I were left in the back of the room on a hard bench. At the front of the room were two tables with chairs, one table on each side of the room. On the left were twelve chairs fenced in like a box. On the right side near the front wall were a table and chair raised up so that the person in the chair could be seen.

People, mostly men, gathered slowly. I heard them greeting each other outside, but as they entered the room, they became quiet. Some looked at me and Little Bett as if surprised, but

they said nothing. An occasional cough was the
only sound. What had happened to Bett and
Brom? I wondered.

Suddenly a door opened, and Bett and Brom
with lawyers Sedgwick and Reeve came into the
room and sat at the table near the twelve seats.
Then the master and mistress came in with their
lawyers and sat on the opposite side. She wore
a soft voile dress with small black-and-white
dots, and a large white hat with bright red flowers, and red shoes. The master wore a white
suit. There was a flutter of greetings in the room
when they arrived. Soon a banging noise from
a wooden mallet sounded and a booming voice
said, "All rise!"

Little Bett and I stood with the others until
a small man with a beaklike nose entered the
room. He was wearing a long black robe and a
white wig with big curls that almost covered his
face. When he sat in the raised chair, we were
asked to be seated.

Things began to happen right away. Lawyers
Noble and Canfield called for a dismissal of the
case on the grounds that "the said Brom and
Bett, are and were at the time of the original
writ, the legal Negro servants of the said John
Ashley during their lives, and the said John

Ashley is ready to verify, and hereof prays the judgment of this court, that the said suit may be abated."

Lawyers Reeve and Sedgwick replied, "This suit should not be abated because Brom and Bett are not legal Negro servants or servants of John Ashley during their lives."

"There seems to be enough evidence to warrant a full hearing of this case. Let us proceed," the judge said.

Men were called from the audience and asked to give their names and tell what kind of work they did. Then Lawyer Sedgwick and one of Master Ashley's lawyers began to ask them questions. Were they property holders? "Do you feel that a person has the right to hold another in servitude?" Lawyer Sedgwick asked one man.

The man replied, "The Bible, the very word of God, says we have the right to hold those who are less than us in slavery, and according to that same Bible slaves are meant to obey their masters whether the masters are good or evil."

Finally they had questioned about seventeen of the men in the room. Three without property were dismissed immediately. The lawyers talked to each other and then lawyer Canfield, for the Ashleys, and Sedgwick, for my sister, talked to the judge. The room was quiet, but the heated talk between the lawyers and the judge could not be heard. Then two more men, including the one who had said God intended for there to be masters and slaves, were told they were not needed for jury service.

When twelve men were finally settled in the jury box, the judge gave them their first instruction: Listen to both sides of the arguments in order to make a decision based on those arguments and not on their own opinions. Then the bailiff of the court stood with papers in hand and read a long statement about why the court was in session. I understood little of what he said except that the master had refused the orders of the court to release Bett and Brom because they were his servants for life. The court was to decide whether or not John Ashley had a claim on said Bett and Brom as his servants for life.

After the reading, the judge turned to the lawyers. "Are the plaintiffs ready to present evidence and witnesses?"

"We are, your honor," Master Reeves said. He moved away from the table and stood between the jury and the judge. "We will be brief.

John Ashley, a well-known citizen in this state, held Brom and Bett against their will in bondage without pay. We intend to prove that under the Massachusetts Constitution and under the Declaration of Independence of the United States, he has no legal right to hold said Brom and Bett."

Then Master Noble stood. "Your honor, we will prove that John Ashley and his wife, Anna Ashley, are kind, caring master and mistress to their servants; that Judge John Ashley, whom even my opponent admits is an upstanding, law-abiding citizen, has the right to hold slaves as property, as do many outstanding citizens, such as our General Washington, and Thomas Jefferson, who helped write our noble Declaration of Independence."

I looked at the twelve men in the jury box and wondered what they were thinking. Would enough of them think like Master Reeve? Or did they think, like Master Noble, that they had the right to keep us slaves forever?

Master Noble called Master Ashley to the stand and questioned him: How had he come to own us? Had he seen to it that we were well fed, clothed, and housed? Had he seen to it that we were changed from heathens to Christians?

The master answered, "Yes, I have." When Master Reeves said he had no questions, Master Noble said, "I call Mistress Anna Ashley."

There was a stir in the crowd as she made her way to the stand. As always, when she was in public, she was confident and assured. She seemed not to notice anything around her, except once to raise her eyes to the ceiling. She mopped her brow, suffering from the heat. "Will you describe to the court your relationship with your servant, Bett?" her lawyer asked.

"Bett is like one in my family. She was born on my father's land and has been a servant of mine even before I married her master. We have never quarreled, and I have been nothing but kind to her."

I was afraid I was going to start laughing, so I closed my ears and mind to her and held on to keep from being tossed out of the place. How could she sit there pretending that she was a good mistress? I looked at my sister, who sat upright and calm, and I wondered, if asked to disagree with the mistress, would she have the will to do so?

Master Reeves said he had no questions for the mistress and called Bett. I could tell that Bett was reluctant. He whispered something to her, and finally she came forward and sat in the seat where the mistress had sat. "Your honor," Master Reeves said, "I would like to prove that the mistress Ashley is not the kind mistress she claims." He then turned to the jury. "The issue here is not whether the Ashleys have been kind. The issue is, do they have the right to hold Bett and Brom as slaves for life?" He turned to Bett. "Has Mistress Ashley ever in any way abused you?"

My sister looked at the judge and then at Lawyer Reeves. She did not speak. The court-room was hushed, waiting. Answer him! I wanted to say. Why didn't she tell them and show the ugly wound on her arm?

Bett looked at the mistress, who was staring Bett in the face. "Yes, Master Reeves, she is not the kind person she wants people to believe she is. I have been in her household many years and was never paid one pence. We work six days a week and sometimes on the seventh. But whether she is kind or not, the constitution says we have rights to our freedom."

"No further questions," Mr. Reeves said.

Master Noble stood and said, "Bett, you sit here well dressed, in good health, with nothing to even hint at your being anything but blessed to be a servant of the Ashleys." There was applause and sounds of "Hear, hear!"

The judge pounded on his desk. "There must be order in this court. Continue, Mr. Noble."

"You know your master and mistress have been good to you, haven't they, Bett?"

"I object," Lawyer Reeve said. "Whether they were good to her is not the question here."

"Objection sustained."

"Your honor, my worthy opponent asked if she had been abused. May I rephrase the question? What proof can you give to this court of Mistress Ashley's abuse?" Lawyer Noble asked.

My sister looked at the mistress, then at the judge. She did not answer. Was she afraid, thinking What if we lost? What would the master and mistress do to us? I felt cold sweat rolling down my sides. In that room that had been almost unbearably warm, I became chilled.

Suddenly Bett squared her shoulders. Without saying a word, she rolled up her sleeve and bared the wound. It was still scarlet with the healing pulling the muscles tight, making the arm twist out of shape, limiting its range of movement. She held her arm so that all could see. There was a gasp in the audience.

Lawyer Noble rushed to the mistress. Lawyer

Canfield joined him, and they whispered in conversation with her. The mistress lowered her head when her lawyer said, almost in a whisper, "I have no further questions."

The judge asked if there were other witnesses and questions. Both sides said, "No, your honor." Then the judge gave final instructions to the jury: "You have heard arguments in this case. You are bound by the law, only by the law, that has been presented here, not by pity and sympathy for either side. It is your duty to determine if the idea of slavery is not in keeping with our own conduct and with our constitution, and that, therefore, there can be no such thing as life servitude of a rational creature." Then he said, "We'll hear your closing statements now."

In his closing statement, Master Noble reminded the jury of Master Ashley's outstanding citizenship. "He is one who sits in judgment and knows the law. Would he break the laws that he so proudly administers? I say no, he would not." He went on and on.

"Gentlemen of the jury, Master and Mistress Ashley have every right to hold on to their servants, as all of our history declares. The Ashleys along with other great men, Thomas Jef-

ferson, our great General Washington, and
many others, hold slaves. Are they not good
law-abiding citizens? They know that these people are not capable of caring for themselves. If
freed, how will they live? Will their freedom
make them wards of the state, so that you and
I will have to care for them? Let Master Ashley
continue to keep his servants, for we all know
he is a good kind master. I rest my case."

The applause from the crowd was hammered
down by the gavel in the judge's hand. I was so
angry and upset that I missed the beginning of
Lawyer Reeve's closing.

". . . There are some things in our history that
Mr. Noble did not dare talk about that have
happened in this very state of Massachusetts
and this Berkshire County. Many of you remember the meeting held in the town of Sheffield where even some of you approved without
a single 'nay' these words: 'Resolved that Mankind in a State of Nature are equal, free and
independent of each other, and have a right to
the undisturbed enjoyment of their lives, their
liberty and their property.'

"One of those men who hold slaves, Thomas
Jefferson, echoed *your* feelings in the Declaration of Independence when he wrote, 'We

hold these truths to be self-evident, that all men are created equal, that they are endowed by their Creator with certain unalienable rights, that among these are life, liberty and the pursuit of happiness.' You continued that idea in your state constitution with a bill of rights."

I was so happy when he told them that Bett was a midwife and Brom a herdsman, who could certainly take care of themselves. There was some laughter when he mentioned how long Bett and Brom had worked and the folly of the idea that they couldn't look after themselves. But the place got real quiet when he came to the end.

"I say that the city of Sheffield and Berkshire County, the first to have a meeting and a petition on ending slavery and on declaring in favor of independence from the king, is no place where a citizen can be called law abiding if he claims ownership of another human being.

"Gentlemen of the jury, make the Declaration of Independence and your state constitution meaningful in our lives now. Declare that no title to a slave is valid, and grant Brom and Bett their liberty so that they may pursue happiness. I rest my case."

There was no applause, but the silence was

complete. The judge waited; no one stirred. "The jury will now convene." He called the bailiff, who escorted the jury to a room where they could decide the verdict.

What would happen now? I thought of the applause when Lawyer Noble said that Bett looked anything but mistreated. What if they agree with the master that he has a right to us as his property? I can't go back to that house. But where will I go?

In spite of my worry and fears, time did not drag, and before two hours had passed the bailiff announced that the session would begin again. "All rise." The judge entered.

After we were all seated, the judge asked the jury foreman, "Have you reached a verdict?"

The foreman replied, "We have, Your Honor."

My heartbeat could be seen in my chest and my hands were clammy with sweat. Oh, God, let them. Please let them say we're free.

"We find for the plaintiffs. The said Brom and Bett are not and were not legally Negro servants of him, the said John Ashley, during life. We further assess thirty shillings, lawful silver money damages."

Did I hear right? I looked at the mistress.

Her face was red with anger. Then I looked at
my sister, who was smiling and embracing her
lawyers. I wanted to join her and Brom up front
to share that moment, but the judge was banging his gavel. "Order, order! I adjudge and determine in accordance with the jury's verdict
that Brom and Bett are free. I accept the jury's
recommendation that the Ashleys pay Brom
and Bett thirty shillings damages. In addition,
the court assesses the Ashleys the cost of this
suit, five pounds, fourteen shillings, and four
pence. This court is adjourned."

Finally, the four of us were together. "We
are free!" Bett cried. "Can you believe it, *free*."
We all four hugged each other and tears of joy
flowed. We cried and cried. Tears for Baaba,
for Yaaye, for Josiah, for Olubunmi, and for
our five brothers, Africa, Cuff, Titus, Quam,
and Prince.

I knew that the status of the child was that
of the mother. Little Bett was also free. There
was nothing said about me. My fear returned
that the mistress had no use for me and would
insist that I be sold.

26

Before we had time to really celebrate, the worst blow that could ever fall fell upon us. Lawyer Sedgwick told Bett that the master had not accepted the verdict and that she and Brom would have to go to a higher court and present their case before they could be declared free.

How could that be! All the old fears returned. We could not sleep or eat. We sat around in silence, feeling that it all had been for nothing. When Sarah came to celebrate the winning of the first round, she sensed our sadness and tried to cheer us up. "I have a feeling," she said, "that the master is going to call this whole thing off. You know Zach Mullen, the quiet, don't-want-to-be-bothered one? He didn't show up for his trial that was also scheduled during the session of this court. Maybe he and the master made a deal out of court. You got the master on the run. Besides, being a former judge, he knows that the Supreme Judicial Court has already ruled for Quok Walker in Worcester. By the time they come to Berkshire County, everyone will know that slavery is unconstitutional." The State Supreme Court would not convene in Berkshire County until October.

That was not enough for my sister. She had heard Master Ashley claim the right of property, and we were his property. She knew that he was an outstanding businessman who had not become powerfully rich by giving away what he owned. And she had seen his strong will against the constable. She continued to work for Lawyer Sedgwick and to hold her head high, but I knew she was frightened. However, Sarah was right.

Two weeks before the second trial, Colonel Ashley dropped his appeal and accepted the decision that Brom and Bett were not slaves. He agreed to pay both of them thirty shillings lawful money damage and the cost of the suit:

five pounds, fourteen shillings, and four pence. My sister and brother were, indeed, free.

Oh, the shouting and praise giving! Friends came with food and congratulations. It was a glorious day. Of course I was happy for them. But my fear was overwhelming, for nothing had been decided about me, and every minute I waited for the master to come and say that the mistress wanted me back. Finally Bett, seeing my gloom, said, "Of all people, I thought you would shout the loudest."

"Why? The master said I could go, but if the mistress so chooses, I must return. Besides, I must pay him for my freedom."

"Aissa, *minyiyo*" — for the first time she called me younger sister in our mother's tongue — "the constitution says that slavery is illegal. You are no longer a slave. *You are free.*"

"Bett, is that true, really true?" I cried.

"It is true!"

All those years I had imagined what it would be like to live those words, *I am free!* Now I didn't know any words to describe what freedom meant, and I didn't try to find any.

Epilogue

Out of necessity, I have shared my most private experiences. I have tried to join my life with the forces of history to create for myself a name, a personality, unique unto me alone. I know that I didn't just happen. I was born; my forebears had names, and a language; they had a culture, a way of life. I now have a name, my claim that I stake against the world. No longer will I panic over going nameless up and down the streets of others' minds. My name is *Aissa*! Bett took the name Elizabeth Freeman and her child became Ayisha.

The question arises, what are you doing now? The master denied his claim on me, but he gave me no money for all my years of servitude. With a gift of money from my sister and brother, I moved to Boston. I have a job in the home of a well-to-do merchant. I live in a boardinghouse with other African women my age.

Boston is an overwhelming town. I am grateful that I can read and know what is going on. With all the worry about our freedom, we didn't pay much attention to the war. But the Colonials won, and the thirteen colonies have now become united states.

Sarah and I keep in touch through letters. She tells me what is happening in and around Sheffield. My sister continues to work for the Sedgwicks. She found no cure for the wife but, Sarah said, "Elizabeth, knowing that the body, the mind, and the spirit are one, brought her mistress great relief. Your sister uses just the right herbs that relax and soothe the nerves, and the mistress can go for months at a time without an attack. It seems as though with Elizabeth's warm baths, special foods, and encouragement, the patient has been able to open up and express how she really feels. She has gone so far as to write her husband telling him how difficult is his being away leaving her alone to care for the children.

"The children love your sister because she's

kind to their mother and accepts her as she is. They all call your sister 'Mum Bett.' "

Each day I give thanks for my sister — *moni ma faatuma debbo* — what a woman! I am grateful to my brother, and to Olubunmi, who gave me life and a guide to live it well; to Sarah, who gave me the most wonderful gift, the secret treasure of words. I give thanks for the lawyers who helped us get our freedom.

Some say that *Brom & Bett* v. *Ashley* was the case that ended slavery. Others say it was *Quok Walker* v. *Jennison*. It doesn't matter. Fact: It happened. Both cases ended slavery in the Commonwealth of Massachusetts and started the long hard road to slavery's abolition.

No. Slavery is not ended. There has been nothing in the papers about these cases; so many people are unaware that the Supreme Court of *our* state has made a solemn decision based on the state constitution and the bill of rights that slavery is illegal. I wonder. How many slaves are out there still not knowing that they are legally free?

Now, for the first time in my life, I can say I'm happy. I am learning to speak Fulfulde, my mother's language. As I walk the streets I remind myself of what Olubunmi and my sister knew so well: Say no to bondage and no one can keep you a slave. And I have now learned that no one can set you free. Freedom is living with realities in a way that they don't overcome you. And as my mother would say, *"Tiigaade! Faa o waawa hoore mum!"* — "Hold on steady! Until we know ourselves, we will never be free!"

Historical Note

The talk of independence and equality that preceded and continued during the Revolutionary War caused many blacks, both as individuals and groups, to petition for their freedom from 1773 to 1779.

One such petition, in the "Province of Massachusetts Bay To His Excellence, Thomas Hutchinson, Esq: Governor; To the Honorable His Majesty's Council, and to the Honorable House of Representatives in General Court assembled at Boston, the 6th day of January, 1773, . . ." was a group petition signed by a black named Felix.

Another, in Boston in April 1773, on behalf of fellow slaves in the province, and by order of the committee, was signed by Peter Bestes,

Sambo Freeman, Felix Holbrook, and Chester Joie. In 1777, the Honorable Counsel of [Representatives] for the State of Massachusetts Bay in General Court assembled on January 13 were petitioned again by a "great number of Blacks detained in a state of slavery in the Bowels of a free & Christian Country. . . ."

During the Revolution, from 1779 to 1784, slaves protested and gained their freedom through service in the war and through the flight of Tory masters.

In the preceding account, Bett's fictional sister, who was between fifteen and seventeen at the time, confesses her role in these events. Where records have been kept of names of people involved, I have taken the liberty to use those names. For most slaves no record of names was found, and therefore I have given names which I imagined were appropriate for newly arrived Africans to the American colonies in the 1600s and 1700s. I have used names that were known in history, but not necessarily for the activities stated here. Although Lemuel Haynes, Agrippa Hull, Felix Holbrook, Salem Poor, and Peter Salem were all outstanding black contemporaries of Elizabeth Freeman, I have no indication that they ever met.

The slave petitions are from Herbert Aptheker's *A Documentary History of the Negro People in the United States*. (New York: The Citadel Press, 1951.)

The opening statement made at the trial for Brom and Bett was taken from an account of the trial in the *William And Mary Quarterly*, Third Series, Vol. XXV, No. 4, October 1968.

My thanks to Milton Meltzer, who shared the many pages of research that he had done on this subject, and to Jacqueline Middlehoek-Sainsbury for her help with the Dutch language, and to David Abdula for sharing his Fulfulde language.